The Iguana Killer
Twelve Stories of the Heart

The Iguana Killer

Twelve Stories of the Heart

Alberto Alvaro Ríos

Etchings by Antonio Pazos

A Blue Moon and Confluence Press Book

2/1985
gen'l

WINNER OF THE 1984 WESTERN STATES
BOOK AWARD IN SHORT FICTION

Sponsored by the Western States Arts Foundation in Santa Fe, New Mexico, The Western States Book Awards are presented to outstanding authors and publishers of fiction, short fiction, creative non-fiction, and poetry. Jurors for 1984 were Robert Penn Warren, Jonathan Galassi, Carolyn Kizer, Al Young, and Jack Shoemaker. The Western States Arts Foundation Book Awards are organized by the Western States Arts Foundation with funding from The Xerox Foundation, the B. Dalton Bookseller, and the National Endowment for the Arts.

Earlier versions of these stories have appeared in the anthology, *NEW AMERICA: Cuentos Chicanos,* and the following journals: *Blue Moon News; De Colores: The Best of Chicano Fiction; The Mendocino Review; New Times; Salt Cedar,* and *Revista Chicano-Riquena.*

"The Way Spaghetti Feels" was a winner of the *New Times Fiction Award;* "The Iguana Killer," "The Child," "Pato," "His Own Key," and "A Friend, Brother Maybe" were the featured stories in a special issue, *De Colores: The Best of Chicano Fiction,* which came as a result of being a finalist in *The Pajarito Premio Award.*

The author extends special thanks to Peggy Shumaker for her help in editing, and to Lupita, who lived through these stories and all the times they have changed.

Publication of *The Iguana Killer* is made possible, in part, by the Arizona Commission on the Arts, a State Agency, the National Endowment for the Arts in Washington, D.C., a Federal Agency, Western States Arts Foundation, and Confluence Press at Lewis-Clark State College in Lewiston, Idaho. The publisher also acknowledges the generous and long-standing individual patronage of Clint Colby.

ISBN: Cloth 0-933188-28-5   Paper: 0-933188-29-3

Distributed to the trade by: Kampmann & Company, Inc., 9 East 40 Street, New York 10016.

For Agnes and Alberto, my mother and father.
The ten dollars a week back then, it was exactly enough.

No one ever keeps a secret so well as a child.

Victor Hugo

Contents

The Iguana Killer

Sapito had turned eight two weeks before and was, at this time, living in Villahermosa, the capital city of Tabasco. He had earned his nickname because his eyes bulged to make him look like a frog, and besides, he was the best fly-catcher in all Villahermosa. This was when he was five. Now he was eight, but his eyes still bulged and no one called him anything but "Sapito."

Among their many duties, all the boys had to go down to the Río Grijalva every day and try to sell or trade off whatever homemade things were available and could be carried on these small men's backs. It was also the job of these boys to fish, capture snails, trick tortoises, and kill the iguanas.

Christmas had just passed, and it had been celebrated as usual, very religious with lots of candle smoke and very solemn church masses. There had been no festivities yet, no laughing, but today would be different. Today was the fifth of January, the day the children of Villahermosa wait for all year. Tomorrow would be the *Día de los Reyes Magos,* the Day of the Wise Kings, when presents of all sorts were brought by the Kings and given to friends. Sapito's grandmother, who lived in Nogales in the United States, had sent him two packages. He had seen them, wrapped in blue paper with bearded red clown faces. Sapito's grandmother always sent presents to his family, and she always seemed to know just what Sapito would want, even though they had never met.

That night, Sapito's mother put the packages under the bed where he slept. It was not a cushioned bed, but rather, a hammock, made with soft rattan leaves. Huts in Villahermosa were not rented to visitors by the number of rooms, but, instead, by the number of hooks in each place. On

1

these hooks were hung the hammocks of a family. People in this town were born and nursed, then slept and died in these hanging beds. Sapito could remember his grandfather, and how they found him one afternoon after lunch. They had eaten mangoes together. Sapito dreamed about him now, about how his face would turn colors when he told his stories, always too loud.

When Sapito woke up, he found the packages. He played up to his mother, the way she wanted, claiming that the *Reyes* had brought him all these gifts. *Look and look, and look here!* he shouted, but this was probably the last time he would do this, for Sapito was now eight, and he knew better, but did not tell. He opened the two packages from Nogales, finding a baseball and a baseball bat. Sapito held both gifts and smiled, though he wasn't clearly sure what the things were. Sapito had not been born in nor ever visited the United States, and he had no idea what baseball was. He was sure he recognized and admired the ball and knew what it was for. He could certainly use that. But he looked at the baseball bat and was puzzled for some seconds.

It was an iguana-killer. *"¡Mira, mamá! un palo para matar iguanas!"* It was beautiful, a dream. It was perfect. His grandmother always knew what he would like.

In Villahermosa, the jungle was not far from where Sapito lived. It started, in fact, at the end of his backyard. It was not dense there, but one could not walk far before a machete became a third hand, sharper, harder, more valuable than the other two in this other world that sometimes kept people.

This strong jungle life was great fun for a boy like Sapito, who especially enjoyed bringing coconuts out of the tangled vines for his mother. He would look for monkeys in the fat palm trees and throw rocks at them, one after the other. To get back, the monkeys would throw coconuts back at him, yelling terrible monkey-words. This was life before the iguana-killer.

Every day for a week after he had gotten the presents, Sapito would walk about half a mile east along the Río Grijalva with Chachi, his best friend. Then they would cut straight south into the hair of the jungle.

There is a correct way to hunt iguanas, and Sapito had been well-skilled even before the bat came. He and Chachi would look at all the trees until the tell-tale movement of an iguana was spotted. When one was found, Sapito would sit at the base of the tree, being as quiet as possible, with baseball bat held high and muscles stiff.

The female iguana would come out first. She moved her head around very quickly, almost jerking, in every direction. Sapito knew that she was not the one to kill. She kept the little iguanas in supply—his father had told him. After a few seconds, making sure everything was safe, she would return to the tree and send her husband out, telling him there was nothing to worry about.

The male iguana is always slower. He comes out and moves his head to one side and just stares, motionless, for several minutes. Now Sapito knew that he must take advantage, but very carefully. Iguanas can see in almost all directions at once. Unlike human eyes, both iguana eyes do not have to center in on the same thing. One eye can look forward, and one backward, like a clown, so that they can detect almost any movement. Sapito knew this and was always careful to check both eyes before striking. Squinting his own eyes which always puffed out even more when he was excited, he would not draw back his club. That would waste time. It was already kept high in the air all these minutes. When he was ready, he would send the bat straight down as hard and as fast as he could. Just like that. And if he had done all these things right, he would take his prize home by the tail to skin him for eating that night.

Iguanas were prepared like any other meat, fried, roasted, or boiled, and they tasted like tough chicken no matter which way they were done. In Tabasco, and especially in Villahermosa, iguanas were eaten by everybody all the time, even tourists, so hunting them was very popular. Iguana was an everyday supper, eaten without frowning at such a thing, eating lizard. It was not different from the other things eaten here, the turtle eggs, *cahuamas,* crocodile meat, river snails. And when iguanas were killed, nobody was supposed to feel sad. Everybody's father said so. Sapito did, though, sometimes. Iguanas had puffed eyes like his.

But, if Sapito failed to kill one of these iguanas, he would run away as fast as he could—being sad was the last thing he would think of. Iguanas look mean, they have bloodshot eyes, and people say that they spit blood. Sapito and his friends thought that, since no one they knew had ever been hurt by these monsters, they must not be so bad. This was what the boys thought in town, talking on a summer afternoon, drinking coconuts. But when he missed, Sapito figured that the real reason no one had ever been hurt was that no one ever hung around afterward to find out what happens. Whether iguanas were really dangerous or not, nobody could say for certain. Nobody's parents had ever heard of an iguana hurting anyone, either. The boys went home one day and asked. So, no one worried, sort of, and iguanas were even tamed and kept as pets by the old sailors in Villahermosa, along with the snakes. But only by the sailors.

The thought of missing a hit no longer bothered Sapito, who now began carrying his baseball bat everywhere. His friends were impressed more by this than by anything else, even candy in tin boxes, especially when he began killing four and five iguanas a day. No one could be that good. Soon, not only Chachi, but the rest of the boys began following Sapito around constantly just to watch the scourge of the iguanas in action.

By now, the bat was proven. Sapito was the champion iguana-provider, always holding his now-famous killer-bat. All his friends would come to copy it. They would come every day asking for measurements and questioning him as to its design. Chachi and the rest would then go into the jungle and gather fat, straight roots. With borrowed knives and machetes, they tried to whittle out their own iguana-killers, but failed. Sapito's was machine made, and perfect.

This went on for about a week, when Sapito had an idea that was to serve him well for a long time. He began renting out the killer-bat for a *centavo* a day. The boys said yes yes right away, and would go out and hunt at least two or three iguanas to make it worth the price, but really, too, so that they could use the bat as much as possible.

For the next few months, the grown-ups of Villahermosa hated Sapito and his bat because all they ate was iguana. But Sapito was proud. No one would make fun of his bulging eyes now.

Sapito was in Nogales in the United States visiting his grandmother for the first time, before going back to Tabasco, and Villahermosa. His family had come from Chiapas on the other side of the republic on a relative-visiting vacation. It was still winter, but no one in Sapito's family had expected it to be cold. They knew about rain, and winter days, but it was always warm in the jungle, even for these things.

Sapito was sitting in front of the house on Sonoita Avenue, on the sidewalk. He was very impressed by many things in this town, especially the streetlights. Imagine lighting up the inside *and* the outside. It would be easy to catch animals at night here. But most of all, he was impressed by his rather large grandmother, whom he already loved very much. He had remembered to thank her for the iguana-killer and the ball. She had laughed and said, *"Por nada, hijo."* As he sat and thought about this, he wrapped the two blankets he had brought outside with him tighter around his small body. Sapito could not understand or explain to himself that the weather was cold and that he had to feel it, everyone did, even him. This was almost an unknown experience to him since he had never been out of the tropics before. The sensation, the feeling of cold, then, was very strange, especially since he wasn't even wet. It was actually hurting him. His muscles felt as if he had held his bat up in the air for an hour waiting for an iguana. Of course, Sapito could have gone inside to get warm near the wood-burning stove, but he didn't like the smoke or the smell of the north. It was a different smell, not the jungle.

So Sapito sat there. Cold had never been important in his life before, and he wasn't going to let it start now. With blankets he could cover himself up and it would surely pass. Covered up for escape, he waited for warmness, pulling the blankets over his head. Sometimes he would put out his foot to see if it was okay yet, the way the lady iguana would come out first.

Then, right then in one fast second, Sapito seemed to feel, with his foot on the outside, a very quiet and strange moment, as if everything had slowed. He felt his eyes bulge when he scrunched up his face to hear better. Something scary caught hold of him, and he began to shiver harder. It was different from just being cold, which was scary enough. His heartbeat was pounding so much that he could feel it in his eyes.

He carefully moved one of the blankets from his face. Sapito saw the sky falling, just like the story his grandmother had told him the first day they had been there. He thought she was joking, or that she didn't realize he was already eight, and didn't believe in such things anymore.

Faster than hitting an iguana Sapito threw his blankets off, crying as he had not cried since he was five and they had nicknamed him and teased him. He ran to the kitchen and grabbed his mother's leg. Crying and shivering, he begged, "¡Mamá, por favor, perdóneme!" He kept speaking fast, asking for forgiveness and promising never to do anything wrong in his life ever again. They sky was falling, but he had always prayed, really he had.

His mother looked at him and at first could not laugh. Quietly, she explained that it was *nieve*, snow, that was falling, not the sky. She told him not to be afraid, and that he could go out and play in it, touch it, yes.

Sapito still didn't know exactly what this *nieve* was, but now his mother was laughing and didn't seem worried. In Villahermosa, *nieve* was a good word, it meant ice cream. There was a *nieve* man. Certainly the outside wasn't ice cream, but the white didn't really look bad, he thought, not really. It seemed, in fact, to have great possibilities. Sapito went back outside, sitting again with his blankets, trying to understand. He touched it, and breathed even faster. Then, closing his eyes, which was not easy, he put a little in his mouth.

Sapito's family had been back in Villahermosa for a week now. Today was Sunday. It was the custom here that every Sunday afternoon, since there were no other amusements, the band would play on the *malecón,* an area something like a park by the river, where the boats were all loaded.

Each Sunday it was reserved for this band—that is, the group of citizens that joined together and called themselves a band. It was a favorite time for everyone, as the paddle boat lay resting on the river while its owner played the trumpet and sang loud songs. The instruments were all brass, except for the marimba, which was the only sad sounding instrument. Though it was hit with padded drumsticks, its song was quiet, hidden, always reserved for dusk. Sapito had thought about the marimba as his mother explained about snow. Her voice had its sound for the few minutes she spoke, and held him. Before the marimba, before dusk, however, the brass had full control.

As dusk came, it was time for the *verbenas,* when the girls, young and old, would come in and walk around the park in one direction and the boys would walk the opposite way, all as the marimba played its songs easily, almost by itself. On these Sundays no one was a man or a woman. They were all boys and girls, even the women who always wore black. This was when all the flirting and the smiling of smiles bigger than people's faces took place. Sapito and Chachi and the rest of the smaller boys never paid attention to any of this, except sometimes to make fun of someone's older sister.

An old man, Don Tomasito, the baker, played the tuba. When he blew into the huge mouthpiece, his face would turn purple and his thousand wrinkles would disappear as his skin filled out. Sapito and his friends would choose by throwing fingers, and whoever had the odd number thrown out, matching no one else, was chosen to do the best job of the day. This had become a custom all their own. The chosen one would walk around in front of Don Tomasito as he played, and cut a lemon. Then slowly, very slowly, squeeze it, letting the juice fall to the ground. Don Tomasito's lips would follow.

On this first Sunday afternoon after he had returned, Sapito, after being chased by Señor Saturnino Cantón, who was normally the barber but on Sunday was the policeman, pulled out his prize. Sapito had been preparing his friends all day, and now they were yelling to see this new surprise. This was no iguana-killer, but Sapito hoped it would have the same effect.

Some of the people in Villahermosa used to have photographs of various things. One picture Sapito had particularly remembered. Some ladies of the town, who always made their own clothes, once had a picture taken together. They were a group of maybe ten ladies, in very big dresses and hats, some sitting and some standing. What Sapito recalled now was that they were all barefoot. They were all very serious and probably didn't think of it, but now, Sapito, after traveling to the north and seeing many pictures at his grandmother's house, thought their bare feet were very funny, even if shoes were hard to get and couldn't be made like dresses could. Sapito knew about such things now. He remembered that people in Nogales laughed at him when he was barefoot in the snow.

But now, Sapito had a photograph, too. This was his surprise. Well, what it was, really, was a Christmas card picturing a house with lots of snow around. He had gotten the picture from his grandmother and had taken great care in bringing it back home. He kept the surprise under his shirt wrapped in blue paper against his stomach, so it would stay flat. Here was a picture of the *nieve,* just like he had seen for himself, except there was a lot more of it in the picture. An awful lot more.

At the end of this Sunday, making a big deal with his small hands, he showed this prize to his friends, and told them that *nieve,* which means both snow and ice cream in the Spanish of those who have experienced the two, would fall from the sky in Nogales. Any time at all. His bulging eyes widened to emphasize what he was saying, and he held his bat to be even more convincing.

No one believed him.

"Pues, miren, ¡aquí está!" He showed them the picture, and added now that it was a picture of his grandmother's house where he had just visited.

When Chachi asked, as Sapito had hoped, if it came down in flavors, he decided that he had gone this far, so why not. *"Vainilla,"* he stated.

As the months went by, so did new stories, and strawberry and pistachio, and he was pretty sure that they believed him. After all, none of them had ever been up north. They didn't know the things Sapito knew. And besides, he still owned the iguana-killer.

Three months after the snow-picture stories had worn off, Señora Casimira, with the help of the town midwife, had a baby girl. The custom here was that mother and baby didn't have to do any work for forty days. No one ever complained. Mostly the little girls would help in the house, doing the errands that were not big enough to bother the boys or the big girls with. They'd throw water out front to quiet the dust. Neighbors would wash the clothes.

For the boys, usually because they could yell louder and didn't want to work with the girls, their job was to go and bring charcoal from the river, to bring bananas and coconuts, and whatever other food was needed. Every morning Sapito and his friends would stand outside the door of Señora Casimira's house, with luck before the girls came, and call in to her, asking if she needed anything. She would tell them yes or no, explaining what to bring if something was necessary.

Spring was here now, and today was Saturday. Sapito thought about this, being wise in the way of seasons now, as he looked down on the Casimira *choza,* the palm-thatched hut in which they lived. Señor Casimira was sure to be there today, he figured. There was no need to hang around, probably. Sapito had saved a little money from renting the killer-bat, and he suggested to his friends that they all go to Puerto Alvarado on the paddle boat. They were hitting him on the back and laughing yes! even before he had finished.

The Río Grijalva comes down from the Sierra Madre mountains, down through the state of Tabasco, through Villahermosa, emptying through Puerto Alvarado several miles north into the Gulf of Mexico. The boys looked over at the Casimira *choza,* then backward at this great river, where the paddle boat was getting ready to make its first trip of the day to Puerto Alvarado. They ran after it, fast enough to leave behind their shadows.

Sapito and his friends had been in Alvarado for about an hour when they learned that a *cahuama,* a giant sea turtle, was near by. They were on the rough beach, walking toward the north where the rocks become huge. Some palm trees nodded just behind the beach, followed by the jungle, as always. Sometimes Sapito thought it followed him, always moving closer.

Climbing the mossy rocks, Chachi was the one who spotted the *cahuama.* This was strange because the turtles rarely came so close to shore. In Villahermosa, and Puerto Alvarado, the money situation was such that anything the boys saw, like iguanas or the *cahuama,* they tried to capture. They always tried hard to get something for nothing, and here was their chance—not to mention the adventure involved. They all ran together with the understood intention of dividing up the catch.

They borrowed a rope from the men who were working farther up the shore near the palm trees. *"¡Buena suerte!"* one of the men called, and laughed. Sapito and Chachi jumped in a *cayuco,* a kayak built more like a canoe, which one of the fishermen had left near shore. They paddled out to the floating turtle, jumped out, and managed to get a rope tied around its neck right off. Usually, then, a person had to hop onto the back of the *cahuama* and let it take him down into the water for a little while. Its burst of strength usually went away before the rider drowned or let go. This was the best fun for the boys, and a fairly rare chance, so Sapito,

8

who was closest, jumped on to ride this one. He put up one arm like a tough cowboy. This *cahuama* went nowhere.

The two boys climbed back into the *cayuco* and tried to pull the turtle, but it still wouldn't budge. It had saved its strength, and its strong flippers were more than a match for the two boys now. Everyone on shore swam over to help them after realizing that yells of how to do it better were doing no good. They all grabbed a part of the rope. With pure strength against strength, the six boys sweated, but finally out-pulled the stubborn *cahuama,* dragging it onto the shore. It began flopping around on the sand until they managed to tip it onto its back. The turtle seemed to realize that struggling was a waste of its last fat-man energy, and started moving like a slow motion robot, fighting as before but, now, on its back, the flippers and head moved like a movie going too slow.

The *cahuama* had seemed huge as the boys were pulling it, fighting so strong in the water, but it was only about three feet long when they finally took a breath and looked. Yet, they all agreed, this *cahuama* was very fat. It must have been a grandfather.

Chachi went to call one of the grown-ups to help. Each of the boys was sure that he could kill a *cahuama* and prepare it, but this was everybody's, and they wanted it cut right. The men were impressed as the boys explained. The boys were all nervous. Maybe not nervous—not really, just sometimes they were sad when they caught *cahuamas* because they had seen what happens. Like fish, or iguanas, but bigger, and bigger animals are different. Sad, but they couldn't tell anyone, especially not the other boys, or the men. Sapito looked at their catch.

These sailors, or men who used to be sailors, all carried short, heavy machetes, specially made for things taken from the sea. Chachi came back with a man who already had his in hand. The blade was straight because there was no way to shape metal, no anvil in Alvarado. The man looked at Sapito. *"Préstame tu palo,"* he said, looking at Sapito's iguana-killer. Sapito picked it up from where he had left it and handed it to the man, carefully. The fisherman beat the turtle on the head three times fast until it was either dead or unconscious. Then he handed the bat back to Sapito, who was sort of proud, and sort of not.

The man cut the *cahuama's* head off. Some people eat the head and its juice, but Sapito and his friends had been taught not to. No one said anything as it was tossed to the ground. The flippers continued their robot motion.

He cut the side of the turtle, where the underside skin meets the shell. He then pulled a knife out of his pocket, and continued where the machete had first cut, separating the body of the turtle from the shell. As he was cutting he told the boys about the freshwater sac that *cahuamas* have, and how, if they were ever stranded at sea, they could drink it. They had heard the story a hundred times, but nobody knew anybody who really did it. The boys were impatient. Then he separated the underpart from the inside meat, the prize. It looked a little redder than beef. The fins were then cut off—someone would use their leather sometime later.

The man cut the meat into small pieces. The boys took these pieces and washed them in salt water to make the meat last longer. Before cooking them, they would have to be washed again, this time in fresh water to get all the salt off. In the meantime, the saltwater would keep the meat from spoiling. One time Sapito forgot, or really he was in too much of a hurry, and he took some *cahuama* home but forgot to tell his mother. It changed colors, and Sapito had to go get some more food, with everybody mad at him. The boys knew that each part of the *cahuama* was valuable, but all they were interested in now was what they could carry. This, of course, was the meat.

The man gave each of the boys some large pieces, and then kept most of it for himself. The boys were young, and could not argue with a grownup. They were used to this. The fisherman began to throw the shell away.

"*No, por favor, damelo,*" Sapito called to him. The man laughed and handed the shell to Sapito, who put his pieces of meat inside it and, with the rest of the boys, wandered back to the river to wait for the paddle boat. The shell was almost too big for him. The boys were all laughing and joking, proud of their accomplishment. They asked Sapito what he was going to do with the shell, but he said that he wasn't sure yet. This wasn't true. Of course, he was already making big, very big, plans for it.

They got back early in the afternoon, and everyone went home exhausted. Sapito, before going home, went into the jungle and gathered some green branches. He was not very tired yet—he had a new idea, so Sapito spent the rest of the afternoon polishing the shell with sand and the hairy part of some coconuts, which worked just like sandpaper.

When it was polished, he got four of the best branches and whittled them to perfection with his father's knife. Sapito tied these into a rectangle using some *mecate,* something in between rope and string, which his mother had given him. The shell fit halfway down into the opening of the rectangle. It was perfect. Then, onto this frame, he tied two flat, curved branches across the bottom at opposite ends. It moved back and forth

10

like a drunk man. He had made a good, strong crib. It worked, just right for a new-born baby girl.

Sapito had worked hard and fast with the strength of a guilty conscience. Señora Casimira just might have needed something, after all. It was certainly possible that her husband might have had to work today. All the boys had known these facts before they had left, but had looked only at the paddle boat—and it had waved back at them.

Sapito took the crib, hurrying to beat the jungle dusk. Dusk, at an exact moment, even on Sundays, owned the sky and the air in its own strange way. Just after sunset, for about half an hour, the sky blackened more than would be normal for the darkness of early night, and mosquitoes, like pieces of sand, would come up out of the thickest part of the jungle like tornadoes, coming down on the town to take what they could. People always spent this half hour indoors, Sundays, too, even with all the laughing, which stopped then. This was the signal for the marimba's music to take over.

Sapito reached the *choza* as the first buzzings were starting. He listened at the Casimira's door, hearing the baby cry like all babies. The cradle would help. He put it down in front of the wooden door without making any noise, and knocked. Then, as fast as he could, faster than that even, he ran back over the hill, out of sight. He did not turn around. Señora Casimira would find out who had made it. And he would be famous again, thought Sapito, famous like the other times. He felt for the iguana-killer that had been dragging behind him, tied to his belt, and put it over his right shoulder. His face was not strong enough to keep away the smile that pulled his mouth, his fat eyes all the while puffing out.

11

The Child

The bus station in Guaymas was crowded with friends and relatives of the few people coming or going. The wordless singing of tears, *abrazos*, laughter, and hand-shaking was common on Sundays and Wednesdays. These were the two days that the bus from Mexico City stopped here on its way to Nogales. It was for this Wednesday's trip that the widows Sandoval and García had purchased tickets and had come several hours early to make sure they would not miss the bus.

The two ladies shared a single face, held together by an invisible net, made evident by the marks it left on their skins. They wore black, more out of habit than out of mourning for their husbands, both of whom had been dead for more than ten years. Ten or eleven, it was difficult to say. Time was different now. Each of the ladies carried roughly woven bags with deep purple and yellow stripes. Aside from more black clothing, particularly black shawls, the bags both contained food—lemons, tortillas, sweet breads, cheese, sugar, all gifts. In their free hands, the women carried rosaries made of hard wood and their tickets. On their heads they wore black veils and on their legs black stockings with lines up the back and through which the leg hair showed. These stockings were rolled up just past their knees, worn in the manner of most of the other ladies their age who were at the bus station just then.

The bus arrived at about eleven-thirty and was not yet running too far off schedule. Some of the people coming from Mexico City got off to stretch, but the majority remained. The widows Sandoval and García said goodbyes to those who had come with them, crossed themselves, and got on the bus, which was not crowded this Wednesday, not as crowded as on Sundays, when people had to stand in the aisle. The two ladies found a pair of seats near the back. It took them some time to get the seats because bags and suitcases cluttered the aisle. Their own bags were stretched beyond their original intentions and knocked into people, especially the men who wore straw cowboy hats with wide brims for traveling. After many *excuse me's* and *con permiso's,* the ladies got to their places. Although they had gotten on first, they were the last to get settled. Both were shaped like large eggs, formless and mostly bottom-halved, so bus seats never seemed to be quite big enough.

The bus driver with green-tinted glasses and a thin-thin moustache watched and waited with much patience until they were accommodated to start the bus. As it pulled away, relatives and friends waved and shouted last minute messages, very long, but the two ladies even after considerable effort could not get their window open. The embarrassment was short-lived as smoke from the bus soon covered their view.

The two women were uncommonly quiet as the bus hurtled along. Mrs. Sandoval looked out the window and fanned herself with a magazine she had already read many times, the kind with brown pictures on newsprint that never gets thrown away. Mrs. García, the more talkative and gossipy of the two, held her brown bead rosary and looked around at the other people. In front of her she could see only the backs of heads and cowboy hats. One little girl, her lips white from candy, was standing up on a seat and looking back at her. Across the aisle a man sat pulling a blanket around the head of a little boy. The boy was asleep, and Mrs. García was envious because she had always found sleeping on a bus impossible. Behind her sat another man with a cowboy hat who was reading a magazine. Brown pictures on newsprint. The other few seats were empty.

It was almost noon now, and the bus was getting very hot. The black clothes of the two ladies did not help matters, but they had grown quite used to sweating. Each agreed, this was their lot. They complained to each other now, after many years of friendship and funerals, only with large sighs. No words. Sometimes they would shake their heads, and this said all the words. Everyone on the bus today seemed uncommonly quiet, not just the ladies, as if these people all knew why the two were making the trip. The man across the aisle began to smoke. Mrs. García sighed, and Mrs. Sandoval understood. The other words.

"Excuse me. Is the child all right?" asked Mrs. García. The man next to her was thin and moved like an ostrich, not smooth but in jerks, so that he almost could not light the newest in a line of cigarettes he had kept in his hand. He had green-tinted glasses on, too.

"Well, no, he is sick," answered the man. He did not seem very talkative either, like Mrs. Sandoval, thought Mrs. García. One would think the Republic was at war again, or somesuch. Mrs. García waited for more but the man said nothing.

After a few minutes, Mrs. García, as was her habit, asked him, "What is wrong with the child?" Her custom was not necessarily to ask about the health of children, but rather, simply to *ask*.

"I don't know exactly. We are going to see a doctor, a specialist in Nogales, maybe Tucson."

"Weren't there any specialists in Mexico City? I have heard of some very good doctors. Dr. Olvera. Do you…"

"Well, yes, but they have advised me to go to Nogales and see an American doctor. You know."

"Oh, I see, of course," said Mrs. García. She nodded her head to say yes in the other language. He understood clearly, with his head, also.

Mrs. Sandoval nudged her. "You should stop talking so much, you are going to wake the child," she whispered.

"Yes, yes, you are right. Poor thing." More words to the man, "I'm sorry" with her eyes.

"Poor Agustín," said Mrs. Sandoval.

"What?" said Mrs. García. Spoken words were not always understandable.

"Agustín, poor Agustín," repeated Mrs. Sandoval. She raised her eyes to the roof of the bus. Quickly, and back down.

"He has gone to fine things. All we can do is pray for him," said Mrs. García. Both woman gripped their rosaries and immediately began praying. They prayed the rosary several times together. It did not take them long because they had become very fast at it from many dragging years of practice. When they finished, Mrs. Sandoval went back to looking out the window and Mrs. García looked around at the people again.

She decided to talk to the man once more because there was no one else within speaking range. In any language. This time she was careful to whisper.

"Have you been to this doctor before?"

"What? Oh, no. This is the first time."

"I thought you had because I could not help noticing your American cigarettes. They smell different."

"Oh, uh, yes. No I've never been. A friend…" He offered the cigarettes. Mrs. García shook her head. It said no.

"Did you try giving him some *yerba buena* tea?"

"Pardon me?" said the man. He was surprised at her whispering and showed effort in turning his head to hear her again.

"Oh, I am whispering because I don't want to wake, you know, the boy."

"Oh," he said. And yes with his head.

"What I asked was, did you try giving him some *yerba buena* tea?" Eyebrows up.

"Oh, uh, yes, we did." Eyebrows down, clearly.

"Did you try honey and lemon? Maybe with little bit of tequila? That always helps." Still up.

"Yes, we gave him everything, but nothing helps. Really." Brows, if possible, even lower.

"That is very strange. He must be very sick. Does he have a fever?" Still.

"No, no, he gets chills. That's why I wrapped him in this blanket. I think it helps him to sleep better, too, and the doctor said that he needs lots of sleep." The ostrich in his body was uncomfortable.

"Yes, then that is the thing to do, of course. Keep him well wrapped. Chills can be very terrible, especially if you have arthritis. I have this bracelet for arthritis and it helps a little. Copper. It is the only thing the doctor has given me that helps. Dr. Valenzuela. Do you know him? Sometimes it helps the pain I get in my left shoulder, too. And a lot of liquids. Don't they always say that."

"Pardon me?" He almost was not turning his head to listen.

"And you should give him a lot of liquids, no doubt." Lips pressed.

"Yes, yes, that's right. Excuse me, I am going to try and sleep." He smiled a smile faster than the moment he had taken previously to light a match.

"Oh, of course, go right ahead. I hope you can," said Mrs. García. She let go of him with her eyes. She wished that she could get to sleep. Bus rides always seemed to be endless and her neck always ached, as it did now, a great deal. They would at *El Sopilote* soon and she could get out and stretch. She sighed, but Mrs. Sandoval was asleep, and did not hear.

The bus stopped at *El Sopilote,* and some of the people got off. Some were to stay here while the others just got off to stretch themselves. Mrs. García got off, the man next to her, the bus driver, and several of the men with cowboy hats. Mrs. Sandoval, the child, and most of the women stayed in the bus. It was too hot outside, and the women preferred to stay out of the sun in their black clothes. Mrs. García's neck was more painful than the heat, and needed to be walked.

Some rearranging when everyone got back on the bus accommodated the new people who had been waiting. The two widows and the man with his child kept their seats. The man who had been behind the two ladies had gotten off and now no one sat back there.

The bus started up again, and the driving was soon a blur that felt like the times one counts and counts for no particular reason, to a hundred, a thousand. More. Like counting stars, but not giving up, not being able to give up. Mrs. Sandoval was able to half fall asleep. Mrs. García, tired of looking at the desert scrub and occasional mesquite trees, read the magazine that Mrs. Sandoval had fanned herself with earlier. Read it, really, for the third time. The man next to them stared out of his window and from time to time fixed the blanket around the still sleeping child.

Mrs. García finished rereading the magazine and began fanning herself with it. She sighed to no one in particular, to herself, maybe, if only to tell herself how uncomfortable things were. She looked around and wondered with her eyebrows down if all the smoking the man next to her was doing might not be bothering the child. It was starting to bother her, certainly.

"We are going to a funeral."

"Pardon me?" said the man. Mrs. García was whispering again. His neck almost would not let his head turn around, this time more than ever.

"I said we are going to a funeral."

"Oh, I'm sorry." His head said yes, up and down, but he listened actually with the side of his face, since his neck was strong.

"It was this lady's poor brother." She motioned in the direction of Mrs. Sandoval.

He saw, like people sometimes can, without turning his face. "I'm very sorry to hear that. Uh, how far are you going?"

Her eyebrows went up. Good. At last. "Oh, we're going as far as you are, to Nogales." She forgot the smoke. Forgot in the sense of excused.

"I see," said the man. He fussed with the boy's blanket again.

"How old is the child?" asked Mrs. García. She could only see his short hair from her angle.

"Oh, he is five years old." His head nodded yes.

"He will be starting school soon." Her eyebrows made this a question.

With the side of his face he heard the eyebrows rise. "Yes, I suppose he will." He almost shrugged his shoulders. His body was moving so much, just a little but all over, that perhaps it just seemed like he shrugged, or almost shrugged.

"He died of cancers is what the doctor said." Mrs. García turned her head to look straight forward, and sighed.

As if his face were tied by an invisible string, it turned now toward her at the same moment she looked forward. "Pardon me?"

"This lady's brother. He died of the cancer somewhere in his bones." No motions.

"I'm sorry to hear that." Flat.

16

Mrs. Sandoval had heard the last parts of the conversation. She spoke to Mrs. García, "The man has got enough troubles without you telling him ours."

"Oh, of course, you are right. I'm sorry," she said to the man. She turned to him.

And in the same moment, he faced forward. The string had turned slack, and released him. "That's all right, really," he said, more to the seat in front of him. "Excuse me, I think I will move the child to the back. He will be more comfortable if he lies across two seats, I think."

"Of course," said Mrs. García. She moved her bag with the purple and yellow stripes out of the way to say yes as the man picked up the child and spread him out across the two seats directly in back of the two women. The boy did not wake up. The man sat in the closest of the adjoining two seats so that he was still opposite the two ladies, but one row back.

"The child has slept for a long time," said Mrs. Sandoval to Mrs. García.

Mrs. García sighed. She wished she could sleep like that. "Yes, and isn't his face pale though? A little honey and lemon would surely help some. He must be very sick."

"Agustín was such a good man," said Mrs. Sandoval.

"Yes, yes he was." They both nodded up, and down. Yes.

The traveling was like an hour hand's and several more people got on the bus. They had been waiting along the road and had probably come from one of the ranches because the men wore cowboy hats and the women were not used to shoes. The hats were a cheaper quality of straw. The two widows had prayed the rosary again after mentioning Mrs. Sandoval's brother. They would soon be in Hermosillo. That would surely be like a drink of water. It had been a long time since she had eaten *quesadillas* at the *El Yaqui*, remarked Mrs. García. She put her hand on her stomach. Mrs. Sandoval said that she was not hungry. She put her hand flat on the top part of her chest.

The bus stopped in Hermosillo and almost everyone got out this time. One man was too fat, and did not find rising worth the trouble. He was so used to sitting now, he said, to Mrs. García, who asked, that standing felt unnatural, really. He slept sitting, too, because his stomach felt like a horse stepping on his chest when he stretched out on his back. Mrs. García's head said no, God, from side to side, it's too much to bear. But we're like that, aren't we, said her head. She decided she would not offer to bring him anything from the restaurant. She certainly would not eat if she were like that. The two ladies went out and were followed, patiently because he had no choice, by the man who was sitting now behind them.

"Are you going to bring the child?" asked Mrs. García, in all the ways she was capable. They were already outside the bus, and he did not have the boy with him.

"No, I don't want to wake him. He needs all the sleep he can get." The man crushed his cigarette on the ground.

"Yes, of course. By the way, I recommend very highly the *quesadillas* here. No place has *quesadillas* like *El Yaqui*." She smiled.

"So I have heard," said the man. Yes, nodding.

The ladies went into the restaurant. The man said that he would be right in, but that he had to stretch first, that he felt like crumpled paper. He pulled out one of his American cigarettes. Everyone in the restaurant ordered the *quesadillas* without exception. Rumor had made them larger than any of the other choices, had put more letters in their name. Mrs. García felt that it was the quality of the cream in the white cheese. The man came in a little later and ordered the same. Of course, nodded Mrs. García. He sat by himself at a table near the turquoise painted door.

Mrs. Sandoval ordered an orange soda, preferably a Mission if they had any. Mrs. García ordered an *agua de manzana* and a glass of water. The ladies finished quickly and commented on the tastiness of the food. Yes, yes. Mrs. Sandoval had ordered only one *quesadilla* and Mrs. García had ordered three. They finished eating at the same time.

"I think the *agua de manzana* will given you heartburn," said Mrs. Sandoval. "You ate too fast."

"It's very good for the stomach." She was sure.

"It has always given me heartburn. Why did you order the water when you haven't even tasted it?"

"I am going to take it to the boy. He should have lots of liquids." Certainly, on her face. The doctor, after all, had said so.

"Shouldn't you leave that to his father?"

"The poor man is dazed," said Mrs. García. "I don't think he knows what to do for the child. Anyway, a little water won't hurt, and the poor thing hasn't had any since we got on the bus. His throat must be like the road."

"Yes, yes, that is true," said Mrs. Sandoval. "But shouldn't you tell the man?"

"I told him the child needs lots of liquids but, like I said, he is in a daze. Let the poor man eat. Come on, a little water will be a big help for the boy." The two ladies paid their bill and took the water out. They told the *señora* of the restaurant that they would bring the glass back in a couple of minutes. Yes would have been the word in the *señora's* mouth, opened like a question, yes, of course.

The two widows got back on the bus. It was much easier for them since the bus was almost empty. They made their way past the few people, the far man, yes, hello, he was eating *quesadillas* someone had brought, and got to the back where the child was. Mrs. García saw that he was still sleeping.

"Do you think that you should wake him?" asked Mrs. Sandoval.

"It won't hurt him. He needs the water, especially in this heat." She reached for the covers and moved them from his face.

"Ah, this child is cold. His chills must be like ice," said Mrs. García. Her eyebrows.

"Here, let me see." Mrs. Sandoval's hands.

"Wait," said Mrs. García. She moved the blanket so as to rearrange it and stared at the white child. Vanilla ice cream. "Oh, oh my God!" she screamed, and moved like she had put her hands into the flames of a stove, like when she first learned to make tortillas. She was a young girl then. She moved back with the same kind of strength. Mrs. Sandoval caught her as she fell, fainted.

"¡*Dios mío!* Jesus? Help, ah, this child is dead, he is dead!" screamed Mrs. Sandoval in much the same voice as Mrs. García had screamed. Very high. All the people jumped to get over them. Everyone started screaming, and crying. The fat man came. Mrs. García was laid down in the adjoining chairs and Mrs. Sandoval sat with her, crying and clasping her rosary, squeezing it so that if it had been plastic....A man with a cowboy hat—one of them, they were all mixed up—covered the child again with the blanket.

"Get the police, get the police, the Red Cross," yelled the man, too loudly. "Who is this, whose child is this?"

Mrs. Sandoval gasped. There was a loud implication not only in the question, but in the way he grabbed the seat to push himself, once he was aimed. "He's the man's, the man who ate alone." Mrs. Sandoval half stood. Her eyes went through the bus with sharp edges and fast.

By this time the bus driver was calling for the police. The man was nowhere to be found although everyone looked for him. Every person was asking what happened and the bus was an elevator full of voices. Too many, and they bounced into each other. Mrs. García was brought out and lay resting in a bedroom behind the restaurant. Mrs. Sandoval sat with her, praying out loud. The child was left where it was. Nothing moved it.

When the police arrived, the bus stop was much quieter. Too quiet, like it had been too loud. Everyone was sitting in the restaurant. No one could believe it, and where was the father? The Red Cross ambulance arrived just after the police and took the child away. Just picked him up.

The head policeman was trying to get everyone's attention. "All right, all right, who can tell me what happened here? I am the Sergeant."

Mrs. García's name was mentioned by Mrs. Sandoval. The policeman asked where she was and Mrs. Sandoval led him to the bedroom in back where she was resting. The *señora* was fanning her. Mrs. Sandoval pointed with her eyes.

"Mrs. García?"

"Yes, yes, at your service." She would talk. Of course, if it would help.

"I understand that you can tell me something about what has happened here." It all came from his mouth, like a sergeant.

"Well, only that the man said that the child was sick, and when I tried to give it some water I saw that it was dead. The boy, I mean."

"Can you describe the man?"

"Oh, yes, of course." Her eyebrows went up, one a little more than the other. "He was…"

"Well, I would rather you tell me this at the station house. Is that all right with you?" Like a sergeant still.

"Well, we are going to a funeral." Her eyes looked at the floor.

"I'm sorry. It won't take too long, and there are a number of other busses. Where are you going?" Less like a sergeant. Funerals do that.

"To Nogales," replied Mrs. García.

"Ah, yes, certainly there are other busses going to Nogales today." Head up and down. He was a man after all. She felt better.

"Would I be able to telephone from the station in case something happens to keep me?" She kept her head down.

"Of course, yes of course." Not impatiently.

Mrs. García looked at Mrs. Sandoval. "You go on ahead. I should stay and help. All right?" She asked with all her body.

Mrs. Sandoval nodded her head. "Yes, if you'll be okay." She glanced at the Sergeant. "Try and get to Nogales in time. We will all be waiting for you. It's not too far, anyway."

"I will, I promise." Yes.

The policeman told the passengers that they could get back on the bus. After some hesitation—they wanted to know more, they were still hungry—everyone was ready to go.

"Please call if anything comes up. Be careful," said Mrs. Sandoval, as she hugged Mrs. García.

"I will, I will. Go on now." With the tips of her fingers.

Mrs. Sandoval got back on the bus but this time she sat in front. Mrs. García got into the police car. They waved at each other. Both, in the hands they could not see, held their rosaries. If they had been plastic....

Once the bus got going, Mrs. Sandoval could not help thinking about the child. She prayed the rosary almost all the way to Nogales. What tragedies, her brother and then this child, this innocent child. She would wear black for the rest of her life, she decided. Her life would not last so long. This was the least she could do.

At the bus station in Nogales, relatives looking smaller than she remembered were waiting for her. The funeral was to go on as planned. She told them the story of the child and they were all moving their faces in a thousand ways, each in a manner no one else could. They made words, and half-words. And the idea of the father running away, that was unbearable. She gave them the food she had brought.

Mrs. García was still not there by the time the wake was almost over. Mrs. Sandoval could only frown, could not draw her face into comfort. Her face became smaller as it forced itself together, crowding in the lines, making her almost too young. She wondered whether or not she should call the police station in Hermosillo. Mrs. García called before she could make up her mind.

Somewhere out there she was crying. Mrs. Sandoval listened but almost did not, her head moving too fast from side to side, so that some of the words could not find her. *Dios mío, Dios mío* was all that her mouth could say. Relatives came too close around her. What happened to the boy? Doña Carolina, what's the matter? What is she saying? Is she still going to come? Did they find the father? And?

Mrs. Sandoval spoke. She spoke the words of Mrs. García, who had spoken the words of the Sergeant, who had spoken the words of the doctor. More truthfully, she carried the words.

The child was dead. It had been dead for a long time. That is true. But it had also been operated on. The boy's insides had been cleaned out and replaced with bags of opium. They had tested to be certain. Then the boy was sewn up again, put into clothes. Sometimes this happens. This was not the first.

Oh my God, *Dios mío, Dios mío* was all Mrs. Sandoval kept saying, maybe with words, saying just like Mrs. García. Their heads moved from side to side, but not fast enough.

Pato

Pato was a fat little boy and every time he got up in the morning his covers would be all over the floor. Even in winter the bedclothes were too hot for him and they made him sweat as if he were dressed for school, and this sweat smelled. Pato's mother made him take showers all the time but it never helped. Everything that Pato was near began to smell like him, as if he smoked cigarettes. He would always frown when he was teased or even when he was told seriously about his smell but, underneath, he was sort of proud and happy that the smell of sweat became associated with him wherever he went. Pato was glad that this was becoming his most distinguishing feature, that it was taking over. He was tired of being teased about how fat he was, and about how he walked because of it. That, in fact, was how Pato had gotten his name. There was no mistaking the walk of a duck.

So, he was more than glad to smell. At least this had its advantages. It kept the girls away, for one, and any of the other boys would have been very happy with a power like that. And second, it gave him a room to himself, which was unheard of in his neighborhood. When his father had left home, his older brother, Sergio, moved into the room with his mother saying that he couldn't stand the smell even a minute longer. He said that Pato not only walked like a duck, he smelled like one too. Pato felt that it was definitely worth the price. What's more, his particular smell got him into the Vikings. Not only was he in the club but they also held their secret meetings in his room because it was the only place where they could all be alone. It made Pato feel, well this was the only way he could think of it, grown up.

Pato got out of his bed and walked over his sheets to the door. He always kept it closed so that the odors of real cigarettes and car grease would not explore his room. Outside, he could hear his brother talking to his mother and the sound of potatoes frying. He opened the door and went straight into the bathroom to take a shower. He was hungry but he was not allowed to come to the breakfast table without first cleaning up. His brother had been responsible for that. In fact, his brother was responsible for more and more things since he had taken over as man of the house, and these things always seemed to be rules about Pato. Always something new that he would not be allowed to do. Brothers were like that, thought Pato. It was unfair but when he cried no one paid any attention to him, and sometimes he was hit. Just because his brother earned the money he thought he could do anything. The Vikings understood, though. All of them, Wienie, Usmail, and the rest, were older than Pato, but not older than his brother, and they understood for sure what he felt. Everybody had a brother.

"*Buenos días,* Rafael." His mother was the only one who still called him by his real name. Even his teachers called him Pato, trying to be friendly. All he would do was smile, though. They were white, like Americans on TV. If only they knew some Spanish, wished Pato. Then his friends couldn't say such mean things about him in class, or about his mother and his brother. And they would know that a *pato* was a duck.

"Good morning," said Pato. He smiled with a mouth that looked small on his fat face.

"Hey, how was the water this morning, huh? You should do that more often, and with more soap," said his brother. Pato could never tell when he was teasing or when he was serious.

"The water was cold, like always. Besides, you smell too, you do, Sergio. You smell like car grease and gasoline."

"Rafael, be quiet," scolded his mother. "You know that's his job. Now sit down and eat."

"And cigarettes, too." His mother looked hard at him. When she did that it was almost as if her eyes could push him. Pato couldn't win, and he knew it. He changed the subject, still trying to irritate Sergio who was ignoring him now. "Mama," said Pato, knowing he was stepping into dangerous water, "come and sit down and eat with us."

Sergio looked up and stared at Pato with the kind of eyes his mother knew how to use. Sergio was the man of the house now. His mother had her job. They had been through this before, and Sergio always said the same thing. Pato didn't think it was fair.

"Rafael, stop it and eat. You are both going to be late." She never said anything.

"No we're not," said Pato. "We have lots of time." Sergio went back to eating and Pato smiled. He had gotten hit by his father for telling his mother to sit down before. Something was better. This time Pato had won.

Sergio drove Pato to school in the Eaton's Gas Station and Service truck. He claimed that it was almost his, and always bragged that Mr. Eaton trusted him with a key to the station. At least, he used to brag. Since their father had left the house Sergio and Pato didn't talk much. It was almost as if they had never been brothers, now. For the last year they had kept a quiet, the kind Pato knew existed between a father and a son.

The only thing that passed between them this morning was a joke by Sergio. He claimed that Pato's smell was the only thing strong enough to beat up the gas smell of the truck, peewhew! But Pato knew this had to be a joke because the truck never smelled different from gasoline to him. He told Sergio so, and Sergio had laughed.

Pato got to school a little early and went to sit with Usmail in the ramada. Usmail was from Guatemala, but his parents had died and he had come to the United States to live with his aunt, who was also his godmother and so had to take care of him. That's what godmothers are for, he told Pato. He was kind of tall but fat from the lack of jungle. Here there was nothing to chase. Pato thought that they had something in common because of this fat.

Usmail was an important person in Pato's life. When he had first come here, he made everybody laugh by telling them that he had gotten his strange name from the United States Post Office. His name, Usmail, had been stamped on everything important in Guatemala, and he told stories of other boys named Usnavy. Otherwise, Usmail was quiet and mysterious, like somebody else's father. His leadership seemed to come straight from the black part of his eyes and because of this no one ever thought to tease him about his name, or about anything else as a matter of fact. Pato knew about eyes. Because of his eyes and because of the great jungle stories Usmail used to tell, he had been elected president of the Vikings.

As Pato got to him, he was playing with a jumping bug. He pressed the bug's back in and it sat there, stuck in its awkward position. Pato watched. Then, like a jack-in-the-box, the bug jumped two feet into the air, straightening its back.

"Hi, Usmail. Where did you find it?" asked Pato, watching the bug trying to escape.

"Hi. I brought it from home. We have lots of them."

"You should bring some to the next meeting. They would be lots of fun, you know?"

24

"Naw. You stupid guys would probably kill them."

Pato shrugged his shoulders. The bell rang.

"Hey, I'll see you at lunch, okay?"

"Yeah, okay," said Usmail. "Hey, did you bring a baloney sandwich like I told you?"

"Yeah, I did. With mustard."

"Good," said Usmail, and they both went off to their separate classes. Usmail was a class higher than Pato, but two years older. It had taken time to improve his English. A class higher also meant that he was in the same grade with Wienie.

The lunch bell rang. Pato got up, with difficulty, from his seat in a lone corner. It was his corner because he smelled. His teacher had told him to take a bath, and he told her that he did, very often, and he told the principal the same thing, and this was the only solution that they could find. One time they even gave him a bath at the principal's house, but this didn't work either. So, he got his own corner after everyone complained, and a couple of the kids had called him a dirty diaper-baby, and worse. It never really bothered Pato because it made him feel special. He waddled out the door.

Pato spotted the Vikings at the ramada. Usmail was there, and Wienie, and the others. Pato was the youngest, and Usmail and Wienie were the two most important members, so he was always glad to be with them. It made him feel important, more important than Sergio could ever be. Usmail was the president of the club and Wienie was the king and that's why they were important. It was a strange situation, the kind that arises when there are too many leaders and not enough Patos. Pato sided with Usmail on most things. Wienie had kicked him around more than Usmail had.

"*Qué pasa, plebe,*" greeted Pato. They all said hi, and he took his place at the corner. He opened his sack lunch and took out the baloney sandwich wrapped in wax paper.

"Is that it?" asked Usmail, looking at the sandwich.

"Yes," said Pato. "Here, take it."

"Hey, what's going on," asked Wienie. "How come you're giving him your sandwich?"

"Well, he told me to..."

"Shut up, Pato. It's none of your business, Wienie, so keep out of it," said Usmail.

"What do you mean it's none of my business? I'm the king of this club so it has to be my business."

"I'm the president, so don't worry about it."

25

Wienie tried to use his eyes on Usmail. "Well, you're stupid, anyway, Pato. You don't have to give him your sandwich."

Usmail reached for it. Pato didn't say anything.

"Well, you're stupid, anyway, Pato, and you smell real bad today, you know? You're stupid to do what he says."

"Hey, shut up, Wienie. He can do what he wants to," said Usmail in a low voice, like a German shepherd's.

"Yeah? Well the Vikings can do whatever they want to, too, you know? And I don't think we need a president anymore. You just make people do what they don't want to do," said Wienie as he began to stand.

"And all you ever want to do is fight." Usmail stood, too. Pato was having a hard time breathing.

"Yeah? Well that's what fatty here should do," said Wienie, looking at Pato, "or is he too afraid? Or maybe he's too ashamed because his mother and brother sleep together?"

Pato jumped up but could only stand there. His stomach was moving inside, and it was a big stomach. He had been beaten up by Wienie before. "Usmail, tell him...."

"Shut up," said Usmail to Pato. By now, tears had come to Pato's eyes, but no one noticed. Usmail and Wienie were staring at each other like a pitcher and a batter.

"Okay, we'll have a meeting today after the game, then," said Usmail.

This temporarily settled things. Everything that had to be decided on was always brought up at an official Viking meeting. The question of leadership would be brought up. The question of the insult would be brought up. Maybe. Usually, the game was so much fun before the meeting that nobody remembered this kind of stuff by the end. Pato knew this. Tears were still in his eyes. He would have to take the insult. He would have to forget it, too, because everyone else would, just like always. Pato was teased every day about something, but he had learned to live with it. Anyway, the game was *hoyitos,* his favorite. They played it almost every day, but he never got tired of it, except for the last part. It would be even nicer, thought Pato, if today he could win.

Pato lumbered up to the empty lot where the Vikings always played *hoyitos.* He had just come from home where he stopped to leave his lunch sack and can opener. He felt much better, much lighter now. He had only planned to stay for a minute, as usual, but changed his mind and decided to hang around for awhile and maybe tell his mother about the insult. Thinking back, it was easier than Pato had thought it would be.

"*Buenas tardes,* Rafael," his mother had said to him warmly without stopping her sewing, "are you going to go and play today? It's a good day."

"Yes," answered Pato, "we're going to play *hoyitos.*"

"Try and stay calm and not sweat today. You know how it bothers everyone and they tease you," she said.

"Don't worry." Pato went to the kitchen and got some water. He put two ice cubes from the plastic Safeway bag into his glass and swished them around. "I almost got in a fight today."

"Oh, Rafael, why? What happened?" His mother looked up from her sewing as he walked into the room.

"Wienie said something mean to me."

"I thought he was your friend. Did he tease you about smelling again?"

"No."

His mother waited for him to finish.

"Well, he said something about you and Sergio again."

"I've told you never to pay any attention to gossipers. Your father used to tell you that, too, remember? And the things Wienie says, him especially. You know that."

"Yes, but this was different, mama. Wienie, he told everyone that you and Sergio slept together, just like that, mean, and so everyone laughed, you know, like they all knew something, like Sergio was a scaredy-cat or something, afraid of the dark so he has to sleep with his mother." Pato was glad to get it out in one breath, but now the air was empty as if nothing had been said. For a second he thought he had dreamed the words. Sometimes that happens.

"Do you think there is something wrong, Rafael?"

"No, of course not, mama. I know why Sergio sleeps in your room. He's not afraid of anything. He's told me enough times about my smell."

"Then why did you let it bother you? Such a silly thing."

"I don't know, I don't know. They just tease me so much I never know what to think."

"Then you shouldn't play with them."

"I know, well...but, mama."

The conversation had ended then, and Pato felt relieved. Of course, he could not find new friends since these were the only ones that would play with him anyway, but at least he felt he understood them a little better. It helped to talk. They were only teasing him when they said that they were a tough bunch of guys and that they were tough like Marines because they could take Pato's smell, that this was their training. Usmail had said that, but Pato knew, especially now, that Usmail was his friend.

Hadn't he helped Pato this morning? He really didn't mind giving Usmail his baloney sandwich every day, not now. It was worth it. And Pato was relieved to know that his mother and brother were not, well....Sergio was not afraid, no matter what they said. Stupids. Pato remembered the times he had gone to his mother's room to hide from those things that hid in his room. Always he had cried. Sergio could not cry, not like that, not like those nights. No one could.

Pato decided to forget the insult. *Hoyitos* would be good today and everyone would forget. It was a good day, as his mother said. They probably wouldn't even have a meeting today. As he reached the lot wobbling in his own hard-boiled-egg-on-a-table way, everyone yelled hellos. He felt better. Wienie and Moo and Johnny and a couple of others were already there digging the little holes in the ground from which the game got its name, "little holes." The number of holes dug matched the number of people playing.

"Are you in, Pato?" asked Wienie as he walked up.

"Yes, sure," answered Pato.

"Well, that makes four now. I guess Usmail will play when he gets here. He always does, so that will make five. Perfect." Wienie showed five fingers to Johnny, who was digging the holes. "He better remember the ball," added Wienie.

Usmail showed up after the holes were dug, bouncing the little red plastic ball as best he could off the rocks on the ground. "Let's play, well," he said as if he were saving words. Wienie drew a line with his foot about eight feet from the holes.

"Yeah, and you guys keep out of the way," added Wienie for no real reason. No one had ever gotten in the way.

The boys lined up, taking a position in line with their favorite hole. Usmail pushed Pato out of the way, but the moment was silent. Pato changed holes.

"I don't know how either of you plays this game," said Wienie, you're both so fat." Everyone laughed at them, but Pato was used to it and Usmail was anxious to play. He looked up and they all stopped.

The object is to roll the ball into someone else's hole, first of all, and then run to base and back without letting the "hit" person hit you with the ball. If he does, then you are 'it" and you have to try and hit someone else who is not yet safe. The person left holding the ball when everybody else is safe gets a little rock put in his hole. Three rocks means the end of the game, and the real loser.

Wienie went first, and the hollow ball that they always used landed in Usmail's hole. Everyone took off running as Usmail grabbed for the ball. He hit Wienie. Wienie got the ball then and aimed it at Pato. But

Pato was very good: by accident, the second time he had played, he invented a way to play that no one else could use. Everyone laughed seeing Pato fall to the ground, letting his weight work for him, moving him down at the speed of summer lightning so that the ball missed. This was his way, to take out the legs from under himself, and let the planet Earth do the work for him, hugging him to the ground. Usmail was fat, but too tall, so this specialty was all Pato's. When Pato got up, he had plenty of time to come in "free" since Wienie had thrown the ball hard and had to go a long way to chase it. The first rock of today's game was put in Wienie's hole.

The game went on for about an hour, until the rocks in the holes were about equal. Each boy had two rocks in his hole except Usmail, who had only one. Pato had taken a rock on one toss because after he threw and hit Usmail, Usmail tripped him since they were the only two left running and this gave him plenty of time to get the ball and hit Pato. That Pato was fast going down was true, but as far as getting up went, it was almost faster for him to crawl in to base, which he often had to do as the other boys laughed laughs bigger than the sky. Pato looked at the rocks and knew that the rock distribution was about equal because of the keeping of grudges in the game. If someone rolled the ball into your hole on his turn, you rolled the ball into his hole on the next. The boys were not beginners at the game, and the ball did not fall haphazardly.

Usmail's turn came now. He rolled the ball into Wienie's hole, and everybody ran. Wienie was quick, throwing the ball hard and because of that was a good shot. He got the ball quickly but took his aim slowly, this time, for he already had two rocks. Usmail was watching as Wienie threw hard right at Pato. Running, Usmail tripped Pato again so the ball missed him. Pato got up, more or less, and yelled thanks to Usmail because as he went down he had heard the ball whizz just barely above his head.

Wienie started yelling, but everybody got home safe.

"That's cheating, that's cheating, you can't do that." But it was already done.

"Stop being a cry baby, Wienie. You lost, so stop yelling." Wienie looked around.

The other boys started chanting with Usmail, "Cry baby, cry baby." Finally, Wienie calmed down and told them all to shut up. He probably wouldn't have complained in any other game, but this was *hoyitos,* where the loser is stood up against the wall and everybody playing gets three turns to hit him with the ball. Though the ball was plastic, it still hurt enough for the loser to always make some claims about cheating, not just Wienie. Getting hit was embarrassing because sometimes it hurt but everyone had to pretend it didn't. Wienie was no different, but after yelling he finally accepted his position. His only chance was that if any-one missed on any one of the his three shots, the rules required that he must take the loser's place and become the new loser. Of course, the boys didn't plan on missing, and they rarely did.

"Come on, let's get this over with," said Wienie. He walked over to the powdery adobe wall that still closed in part of the lot. It was crumbl-ing most in one spot, the spot that Wienie walked to quickly. He put his face to the wall and his hands on his hips like he had more important things to do so would they just hurry.

One by one, the four winners shot. Johnny first, then Moo, and Usmail. None had missed. After Usmail had made his first two shots, Wienie reminded him that they were going to have a meeting after all this.

"I really don't think we need a president anymore," said Wienie. "Not a president who takes baloney sandwiches, anyway." Nothing was forgotten.

"Shut up so I can concentrate," said Usmail. "We'll see what we need." Usmail hit him with the ball. The plastic made a noise as it went through the air, high at first, but then low and tired out. Sometimes they threw the ball just to hear the noise, but not now. Pato came up next.

"Come on, hurry up, I can smell you all the way over here and that's worse than being hit." Pato hit him with his first shot. "Come on, fatty, hurry up and throw it so you can run home and tell your mother to make lots of baloney sandwiches, that is unless she's too busy combing your brother's hair." Wienie laughed.

Just then, Usmail took a white golf ball out of his pocket. He handed it to Pato.

Pato held it, and realized what it meant. "No," he said under his breath, almost like it wasn't a real word, "no..."

Wienie yelled, "Well, throw it, come on."

Usmail grabbed some of the fat on Pato's side and pinched him. Pato could smell his own sweat. The pinch hurt worse than any ball ever had.

Usmail echoed, "Yeah, come on, throw it, will you."

Pato weighed the ball in his hand. He threw it.

His Own Key

Monday. Its name was the first thing that came to mind on Mondays. Joey yawned, then opened his eyes. He began to shiver but he pushed his two blankets off to his left with a jerk. The room was still dark but he could easily make out the figure of his brother sleeping on the bed.

"*Oye*, booger, wake up." Joey kicked the bed next to his by reaching over with his leg.

"Shut up," said his brother without opening his eyes. Joey decided to leave him alone this morning. Besides, his feet were too cold now to go messing around. Joey sat at the base of his bed and leaned over to the bottom drawer of the dresser, pulling it open. He didn't let his feet touch the floor.

"Joey, are you up yet?" His mother's voice startled him, even though she called him every morning with exactly the same words. Joey knew what was coming next.

"Is your brother up yet?"

"Yes, yes, we're both up," yelled Joey. His brother was still in bed with his eyes closed. Joey knew that his brother would have to get up soon enough, and besides, he didn't have to get up yet if he didn't want to. He was on the afternoon session at school. Joey figured that if it was him in bed he wouldn't get up until he really had to, even if there was a fire and his room was burning up. Even with his brother in it.

Joey finished putting on his socks and rubbed his eyes as he stood. He noticed that his brother had been spying on him but pretended sleep when Joey turned quickly to look at him. His brother couldn't keep a straight face, though, and started smiling in his "sleep."

31

"Oh sure. Get up, stupid," said Joey as he kicked the bed, harder this time because of his shoe.

"Cheeze," yelled his brother, jumping, "get outta here, will you." Joey flipped him a bird and walked out mad the way two brothers act on a good day. The kind of mad that is laughing somewhere inside.

His father was shaving. "Good morning, José."

"Good morning, papa." His father would get angry if he didn't say good morning. Fathers get all weird about some things, thought Joey. He walked into the kitchen and saw his mother feeding the stove. "Good morning. What's for breakfast?"

"Ay, *buenos días,* Joey. Here," she served him a bowl of Cream of Wheat. "The radio said that school busses will start coming ten minutes earlier. Beginning next month." Joey was sprinkling sugar on the mush. "That means you'll have to start getting up ten minutes earlier."

"Chh, ten minutes earlier, chihuahua. Why can't he be on morning session instead of me," Joey said, motioning at his brother as he walked in. "All he does is play all morning."

"Well, Joey, you play all afternoon," his mother pointed out.

"That's different," said Joey, finishing his breakfast as if it were in a glass, holding the bowl with both hands. He stood, stuck his napkin inside his empty jam glass, gathered together all the dishes he had used and took them to the sink. "And besides," he said as he began rinsing, "I like sleep more than he does."

"Then go to bed earlier," his mother smiled. She was in a hurry, too. Joey knew he was getting nowhere, so he went back to the bedroom to get dressed. As he was ready to leave he checked the last minute details. He had his house key and had just picked up his lunch box. Bright green, with his name in Magic Marker neatly across the top.

"I'm leaving," he yelled.

"Hold on, young man. *¿Qué es eso?* A fifth-grader and he can't even button his collar right." His mother fixed the collar and saw that he had his lunch box. "Late, as usual," she shook her head. "Ay Joey." By this time she was dressed in her white uniform. She would be leaving for work soon, too. "Okay, hurry now or you'll miss the bus for sure, *ándale, adiós.*" She pushed him along by the shoulder, but not too hard.

"Bye," said Joey, running down the walkway past his bike. Boy, he thought, when he came home he was going to ride that bike until his legs came off. Well, he'd ride it if he got tired of skating, anyway.

The morning tardy bell rang. School, this early in the morning. The thought wore a silly beard to Joey as he scanned Mrs. Lee's fifth grade class. Only Eddie was missing. Then he jumped out of his seat as some-body hit him with a paper wad from behind. He bent to grab it and clutched the thing in a throwing position, looking for someone to get back at.

"Joey, what exactly are you doing?" Mrs. Lee always seemed to come in at the wrong time. "*¡Cómo eres de travieso!*" she said as she put one hand in the air as if to spank. She had caught him as so many times before.

"Well, I was just, uh, going to throw this paper away," he said smiling. Everyone started laughing. This happened almost every morn-ing, now, and Joey was beginning to like it. He made a big show of going to the garbage can. Doctor J., walking like a panther, circling the garbage-basket.

"How sweet," she said without emotion. "Class, get out your green readers. Today we are...."

The recess bell rang. Joey had been watching the minute hand inch around the wall clock. He couldn't wait. His hands were itching to finish up the baseball game they had started yesterday at lunch time. He had been up to bat, and he could feel the invisible bat in his hands now. Sometimes he rode his bike this way, too, in school.

Joey ran outside with the others, shoving girls out of the way. The game was soon set up and he found himself at the plate carefully choking his bat, holding it as a lumberjack would.

"*¡Mátalo!*"

"Hit it down left."

"Hard as you can, Joey, come on."

Strike one. Phht. He missed the tree. He choked a little more, kept the bat moving in a circle above his shoulder.

"Run!"

"*¡Apúrate!*"

He had hit it solid. He ran as fast as he could, feeling his legs couldn't keep up with as fast as he was running. He made second, breath-ing through his mouth the way he did at the swimming pool.

His friends made a thousand noises, all yes, though the girls playing their own game nearby seemed not to take notice of all the yelling. Joey looked in their direction, sort of. Kind of.

The next batter hit a low grounder down left. Joey ran faster this time and found himself sliding into home, all gravel and bumps, dust exploding everywhere. Joey was smiling until he heard everyone burst out laughing. He looked around and realized that no one was trying to tag him. The ball hadn't even reached second yet.

33

"Stupid *pendejo!*" they all yelled. Joey grinned and proceeded to bow, then walked away with slow, measured steps, nose held like a giraffe's in the air. Everyone reached for gravel. Joey ran and managed to escape, heading for the ramada and laughing so much he forgot to breathe. It hurt.

"Hey, Joey, come here," someone yelled. He looked up as he ran and saw a small group of boys laughing, but low, the way he and his brother did after the lights got turned off. Rene, his friend, was the one who had been calling.

"*Qué pasa,* René," Joey said as he reached them, shrugging his shoulders as men did, as he had seen his father do. "What's going on, how come you guys aren't playing ball?" It was the games that they didn't have to play that they always showed up for.

"Fuck you," one of them called. They all started laughing as hard as they could, harder even. Joey's face gathered its parts, the lips, the eyebrows, the hairline, somehow in its middle. It was a real frown, not like what he gave to his brother.

"Fuck you, too, *cabrón,*" he said and started to walk off. He had a new feeling inside that took away even the strength to shrug shoulders. He tried to raise them to say so what, the way shoulders can, but nothing would move up.

"Wait, Joey." René ran after him. "We were just joking. We were just trying it out."

"Some joke. What's going on here, anyway?" He didn't feel better yet.

"You probably don't even know what it means," said another of the boys.

Joey looked at him as if he were just a wall. "Sure I do." Joey looked away then. "So what?" No movement in the shoulders still. He tested them.

The boy stepped forward. He was blonde and had freckles so a person almost couldn't see his face, as if it had rusted over and he could barely lift his eyelids. Jay. "I told them what it means, Joey. Just like my brother told me, he told me all about it." Jay was always talking about his brother. Football and football and football.

"Told you about what?" Joey was getting hot somewhere in his head, but he wasn't sure why. His head felt too small suddenly.

"About fuck," said René. All the boys had their eyes on Joey. They laughed real low again when René said the word.

34

"So what," said Joey, trying to stop feeling like now he couldn't move his legs either. Couldn't run.

"Ah, he doesn't even know what it means," Jay said loudly.

Joey gave him a squint-eye look, the one his father gave him when Joey had done something wrong. "You're the one who doesn't know. You don't know anything." The other boys were getting edgy, he could tell. Nobody moved. Or breathed it looked like. Except Jay, who moved like a monkey. He couldn't keep still, and kept talking louder than normal.

"Tell him, Jay."

"Show him."

"Yeah," said Joey, "prove it if you're so smart." That was good, thought Joey. Nobody could ever prove anything. It was never even worth trying.

"Okay," said Jay, looking around like an ostrich's head, "okay." The boys used to pick on Jay sometimes because he wasn't Mexican and couldn't speak Spanish. Right now, none of that mattered. Everyone was listening to Jay.

"Okay, well, my brother told me—and he showed me pictures, too—he said that fuck was when a guy gets on top of a girl, well, like on top, and they have their clothes off, you know?" Everybody nodded his head, yes. Somehow they found the strength for this, if nothing else. "And the guy, like he's got to be a fast guy, he gets his thing, you know," Jay pointed down, "and puts it on the girl. She's even got a place there," he pointed down again, "just for doing this, like a jigsaw puzzle. Well he puts it there and it feels real good, you know. And that's how babies are made. Just like that, guy puts his thing on the girl and they get a baby, you know. That's how you were made, too, Joey."

Joey glanced at the girls still playing their game. He had no muscles.

"That's a lie," he said low, which was the only way he could.

"No sir, my brother showed me pictures, and..."

"I mean the part about it feeling good," Joey spoke quickly. "I know that's not true. You know, it can't be." Joey talked too quickly, trying in this way to think. "I mean, if it felt good, guys would be doing it all the time, all of them, and, *pendejo,* there'd be too many babies, you know. It's the truth." Joey ran as fast as he could with his words, any direction, just to keep moving. At least his mouth was working. "That's how come us kids don't go making no babies, know what I mean, cause it don't feel no good. It's kinda like school. Just like school." Run.

"I hate school," said René, "and I wouldn't know what to do with a baby anyway." Joey was glad René was his best friend.

"Yeah. Besides," said Joey, "all those girls wanna do is stupid stuff. It's all stupid. They're dumb, you all know that. Come on."

The bell rang, just as it had on every other day Joey could remember. The children all lined up and Mrs. Lee tapped an eraser in her hand, looking mad, and said they were all late. Just as on every other day. Joey looked around and could find nothing different-looking about anyone. Braids and torn pants' legs and arithmetic books.

But today had to be different, Joey wanted to yell. He felt his stomach scrunched up and pressing backward all the way against his spine but didn't tell Mrs. Lee because she would ask why and he didn't want to tell her that fuck made his stomach cry. He wasn't even sure that was the reason, anyway.

Joey spent the rest of class time thinking about babies, and if they were made. It felt like some super barbell pressed against his neck. Like taking out the garbage sometimes when he really didn't want to but his mother said *right now*.

School finally let out. This last class was an elevator, stuck, with too many people. He thought about his brother when the second session's bell rang. Joey wanted to be him all of a sudden. Little brother.

The bus ride home was just like it was every other day. He felt like yelling again. When he got home he knew that no one else would be there. His brother was in school and his parents were both working. His parents—they had known all along. If it were true, he reminded himself.

Joey walked home from the bus stop. Maybe he had stepped into some Twilight Zone or Outer Limits, those old shows on TV. Everything should be different in some way, but nothing was. One thing, that's all. Nobody else knew anything was wrong.

He reached home. His bike was still there, his skates. Nothing had changed as far as he could tell except now he didn't want to play, not like this morning. His legs were already worn off. He didn't have to ride his bike.

Joey felt for his house key. He kept it tied to a leather strand that was tied to a belt loop so that he wouldn't lose it. All his friends admired the key, or really, just that he had one. Somehow it made him older, and he always kept it where everybody could see. His parents had trusted the key to him last year and he always took care not to lose it. He smiled and remembered when they had given it to him. How come they hadn't told him about the other "it," too? He had said "the word" before, but now he couldn't, not even inside. Something would happen if he did, he was sure, just as if he had let himself imagine his father had died those nights when he had to come home late. Well, maybe they wanted to make a ceremony out of telling him, as when they gave him the key. Maybe they didn't have time yet. For a moment, he felt the way he had when he broke that window to get into the house before he had his own key. They kind

36

of had to give him one, then. Now he wished for the first time, as he felt the leather strap, that he hadn't done it.

Joey went inside, put his stuff on the couch and turned the channels on the TV. Chihuahua, he thought. Nothing on but those stupid talking shows. Ya ya ya. He didn't know anyone that watched them except grown-ups, like his mother when she was sick. But idiot! maybe that's where they talk about babies and that stuff. He began listening for a while as a bald man talked about a movie but he seemed kind of ugly to Joey. He left it on anyway and decided to keep an ear open just in case as he did his jobs, which were to take care of things his brother didn't do. In other words, thought Joey every day, everything. Today he just began.

He made the beds and could only think about his new-found baby-making power. He had been a baby once, and René and all of them. Joey thought about his mother.

Mother. Mama. She must have done it with papa because Jay had said that he was made that way, too, exactly that way. It had to be a lie, he thought. His head felt pinched, the way he put a can in the can opener, opening food for the cats. Or cracked, the way his father shook his hand. They wouldn't do a thing like that without telling him, or without including him, or—he was mixed up. He felt left out, exactly that. But this might not be true after all. Or they were doing it behind his back when they had made his brother. Without even telling him. His own brother.

Joey felt his stomach crawling up his back again, caving in as one of those pictures of starving kids. So they didn't care after all. A golf ball thought hit him on the head, right then. He was going to have to ask his mother about this. She would tell him. Maybe. Or laugh. If it wasn't true....

Joey felt like the mice they caught. How could he ask his mother about fuck? He couldn't say that to his mother, could he? But he couldn't ask without saying it. How would he ask. "Mama, do you and papa do it, fuck?" or "Mama, did you and papa give up fuck because you thought I'd find out?" He couldn't keep saying "it" to his mother. Even to himself. He grabbed his tongue with his hand and pulled the word off.

No, that wouldn't be any good. He couldn't ask her, he wouldn't. They would have told him if they had wanted him to know, anyway. Maybe they were ashamed. He could understand that easily enough. Sure. That was it. Yes.

Still, nothing changed. "It's not," he yelled out loud, "It's not the same, and I know." He yelled at somebody. At his bed. It wasn't really his bed anymore. But it was, too, He was still going to sleep there.

Joey really wished he didn't know. But he was glad. He got up off the bed he'd been sitting on with the cats, even though he'd already made it, promising himself he would never tell anyone. Someone had to know, just as someone had to empty the garbage. He guessed he was that someone, now. The other guys wouldn't remember. They'd forget. He was the only one who remembered exactly where they hid that 35¢. He knew the exact rock in that statue-thing by the road. Someone also had to make babies. He knew that much for sure. Joey would keep the secret as long as he could. He hoped he would never have to make a baby. René was right. Joey wouldn't know what to do with a baby, either. Give it to his mother, he supposed.

A Friend, Brother Maybe

Frankie sat on the thin bed with his legs crossed, staring. There was no noise. The wind-up clock must have stopped again. It was never right anyway. His parents had left him alone when he had started to shout. Mr. Johnson told them to do that. He said that it would be better, that attention would only make little Frankie shout more. Yes, hitting him was attention. Everyone did what Mr. Johnson said to do. He was the social worker, or whatever. He was also the first social worker that had lasted for more than two full months. Frankie was waiting to see him go. He pressed on the knee of his crossed leg and watched his foot come up. He did it again. The machine clicked.

It didn't do anything else. It just stood there like a football player in the middle of his bedroom, bolted to the floor and to the ceiling. Large bolts. The top part was about two feet taller than Frankie and looked like a television screen. It was just out of his reach, Frankie could guess from experience, and stared at him with the blank, black face of an overhead oven sitting in one of the furniture stores downtown. The microwaves in Sears. The color reminded Frankie of the blackboards just washed on Monday. He would leave early to school on Mondays just to be the first to dirty those blackboards up with chalk and spit. Spray paint once. He had spit at this one, too. That's when his father hit him. That's when the screaming and shouting began. Mr. Johnson became angry all over his face for the first time Frankie could remember. The funny thing was that he was not mad at Frankie for spitting but at his father for hitting him. Chh! Mr. Johnson took Frankie's parents out to his car and drove them away. When they had gone, Frankie got up and went to lie on his bed to decide what to do to this oven-thing.

39

The part underneath the oven was what puzzled Frankie. He was not sure what it was. It looked like a big, brown leather punching bag, the kind like in the weight room, and it was loose, maybe full of something, like a piñata. The machine clicked again. One click. As his mother would do with her teeth every time he did something. Frankie waited for what would happen, but nothing did. Already he did not like this fat cousin in his house. It took up a lot of room. It was like Mr. Johnson. Mr. Johnson who thought he was a saint sent to the Chicanos. *Viejo menso,* they were all dumb old men, these social workers sent to his development. They all spoke English better than Frankie or any of his friends. And Spanish, too. That's why they had beaten up the last one before Mr. Johnson. And Frankie, with his *mala suerte,* had been the only one to get caught, as usual. But it wasn't his fault. The machine clicked again. One click. Frankie stood.

He walked over to the machine. It did nothing more. Frankie wondered why Mr. Johnson had made such a fuss over this stupid-looking thing. Maybe it was valuable or something. Something that could be sold. Frankie reached out to touch the leather-stuff. It felt like football skin, like his own skin when he was cold, or...the machine clicked again, twice, and Frankie jumped back.

He looked at it for a second.

Ha ha ha ho ho hee ha ho hee ha ha

Frankie could never have been prepared for this. Anything natural he could have handled, if it had tried to hit him maybe, but this was too much. His pulse scared up to his head and pounded there. It was the feeling of being caught. At anything. Even though no one was there. His knees ran from under him, ran away. Frankie fell to the floor, but ready to spring up with his arms. The machine stood unmoving in front of him, still laughing. It laughed hard and loud, worse than a fist that beats you up. Like the black laughing boxes at the Kress downtown. But this, this did not stop. It was much louder, stronger than batteries. It was like a witch.

Frankie was mad, madder than he had ever been at any social worker. He jumped up and shot to the front of the machine. It kept on laughing, like the high school guys the times Frankie fought them. He covered his ears.

Then he kicked it.

The laughing kept on, but not quite as loudly.

Frankie kicked it again, harder. Then again, and again.

The laughing began slowing like a drunk man's. Frankie bit the leather and turned it in his mouth like when he was fighting and he was biting someone, like the time his father, smelling, came...the laughing stopped.

40

Frankie stood back. His father would have hit him if he had seen. But his father was not here. Frankie looked at the machine. The laughter had come from it, somewhere, he was sure. Yes. Then Frankie kicked it again. No machine could scare him and get away with it. The laughing started again.

Frankie jumped and tackled it. He pounded it with his fists and bit again. The laughter stopped, faster this time. Frankie stood up and looked. The black screen on top was still blank, still had the swish from the wiped spit. The machine clicked again.

This time, Frankie was ready. He was on the offense. Before any laughing could start, he flew into a fight, strong and planned, tougher than Marines. He beat the leather bag until his hands hurt. He kicked and bit like the high school guys and this time the laughing started but quickly quieted. Frankie kept on. But as he did, it began to sob. That was the only word for it. Frankie wasn't listening at first, but the sobbing became a whimper, the sound of a dog that knows it's about to be hit. He had heard the sound before. It was not always from dogs.

Frankie gasped, taking a swimmer's breath. He stopped beating for a minute to step back and look at this thing again. It wasn't going anywhere, after all. He could afford to rest. Frankie noticed the screen this time, and something began to take shape. In letters like the ones above the blackboards in school, the screen formed, "Stop it, please." Like that.

Frankie spit at the screen. Just like a teacher. Or a little guy. Or more, like the social worker they had beat up when he had gotten caught. "Stop it, please." He began hitting the bag again. The whimpering took up, louder. Frankie could not stop this crying, not as he had stopped the laughing. He stepped back, as in the movie with the fat wrestlers.

The screen formed some more words. This time it said, "Stop it, please. You're hurting me." Frankie looked at the message, then started kicking again after clicking his teeth. That was his mother when she didn't believe him. The machine's voice stopped. The screen no longer said anything. Frankie calmed down, remembered to breathe, his hands hurting and, somehow, his ears too. When he hit things hard with his hands, his ears moved up on his head as if they hurt. Like now. He sat back down on the bed. He looked at the machine, which did nothing. Frankie was not about to be outdone.

Sitting like a TV robot on the edge of the bed, staring, letting his muscles hurt, he also did nothing. But he was ready.

"It's only an experiment, of course. Behavior mo..., well, this kind of thing, has a long way to go. We must keep this in mind at all times.

41

Frankie is a rough boy and we hope to make a model of him, but you do remember that I told you this might not work? It should, but…"

"Yes, Mr. Johnson, we remember. We understand. But Frankie is going to break your machine, your experiment. You of everyone should know that."

"Don't worry, it can take the punishment. That's what it was made for, after all. I just hope Frankie doesn't hurt himself. He's a special case." Mr. Johnson smiled and shook hands with Frankie's father. His mother stood behind. She wasn't sure.

Frankie was inside waiting and heard the last parts of the conversation. It was groveling, groveling like always. His father was a *mamón*, an apple-polisher. As if living in the dirt and gin of this unpainted development was a blessing. As if he had to smile and do what anybody with a tie said. As if he were happy. It made Frankie sick, tight-stomach sick. Everyone lived in a development, and they called every one of them "special." But there was nothing special about it. They should ask him.

He was still in his bedroom with the machine. It clicked again. Now it was clicking every so often, and he couldn't guess when. Clicked, as if it were daring Frankie. He could tell. As soon as he heard his parents come in from saying goodbye to Mr. Johnson, he kicked the machine again.

Ha ha ha ho ho hee ha ho hee ha ha

His mother jumped, half-yelling, half-swallowing at the noise, like seeing an accident. *"Madre Santa,"* she said, crossing herself quickly and holding onto her husband. He quickly ssshhhed her. This pleased Frankie, still in the other room where he could hear them plainly through the walls. Frankie's father looked with steel eyes at his wife, Frankie could hear it. Mr. Johnson had said that there was to be no special talk about the machine's presence, and they had both agreed to the plan. It was simply to exist, and to exist only for Frankie. It would be hard. Frankie could hear them not talking, louder than if they had knocked on the door.

He waited for more reaction, for the real knock, but nothing came. He heard nothing until his mother took down the clock and wound it, commenting that it had stopped too soon again. It was very old now. Frankie got up off the bed and walked into the living room. His father kept on reading his Mexican newspaper without looking up. Frankie knew that his father had read the paper at least ten times by now, as he always did. The *Sonorense* was almost his Bible, each issue that his father could get a hold of thumbed so badly that the print was no longer legible. His mother was in the kitchen and made a single noise, the kind that happens almost too quickly, and seems to apologize for itself.

"¿Quieres leche?" she asked, pouring some milk into one of the two glasses on the table.

"No," said Frankie. His tone was familiar by now. His mother said nothing and put the empty glass back on the shelf. No one had mentioned the machine. Mr. Johnson must have done a good job, thought Frankie. He was expecting a yelling lecture about spitting, as soon as Mr. Johnson left. His father still said nothing. Maybe this machine, this intruder, fat pig cousin visiting, would be a good thing after all. And if they would not mention it, he would not either. He was nobody stupid. Nobody stupid at all. He could play this.

The next day caught Frankie the way a push from behind would. It was Saturday, and he would always spend mornings with the older boys, the ones in the Lopers who were mostly around fourteen, in the library parking lot. This Saturday no one was there, not even any of the other gangs. He had heard no news of anything going on or of any plans being changed. Frankie looked around. Only the usual people that really went into the library were there. He went around back and sat on the stoop that overlooked the arroyo. No one came, and it was a long time. Still, maybe he was just early. He sat on the rail and threw pieces of gravel into the dry stream bed below, bouncing them off the concrete sides.

"Hey, Frankie, *qué pasa,* man?"

"Hey, Tony, where is everybody, huh? I been here awhile and nobody's showed up."

"They heard, man. Everybody knows." Tony shrugged his shoulders to say just like that.

"Knows what?" Frankie asked with his head.

"About the thing they put in your house, stupid. We all saw it, you know?"

Frankie looked at him. Tony was older, at least fourteen, and bigger than he was. Too big to beat up. "So what, huh?" He stayed on the rail, sitting so that Tony would not be reminded of his size.

"Shit, Frankie, we all know it's cause you got caught like a *pendejo* when we got that old guy. See, we told you you would. You dumbass, why didn't you run when we told you to, huh?"

"I did." He looked down into the arroyo. He felt like the pieces of gravel hitting the concrete.

"Yeah, but you got caught, man. That's why nobody's here, that's the way it is. We don't want no Mr. Johnson messing around with us like the other one, you know?" Tony jumped over the rail onto the side ramp that led into the arroyo. "I gotta go." He turned around.

"Hey, wait, it wasn't my fault. Everybody was there, I just tripped," yelled Frankie. Tony ran down the dry trail and pretended not to hear. Frankie knew it would do no good to chase him, he was a lot faster. And he had already tripped once, anyway. They were probably around, watching. The word was out, then. No one would come near him anymore. It was like last year with Jonathan J. Whitcomb the Third, who always said his whole name. The whole thing. Jonathan J. Whitcomb the Turd. The Lopers put out the word to ignore him and it was a lot of fun. As if he were invisible. Then his family moved away to the north side because he couldn't find any friends. Now they were picking on Frankie, and it wasn't even his fault. Wasn't.

He started to run home. Frankie didn't know what to do. His family would never move out of the development, especially not to the north side. They couldn't. On the way home he didn't see any of his friends. No one seemed to be out today, not even his real good friends, who could have been out by accident. The game had started. Like signs between a pitcher and a catcher.

When he got home he went straight to his bedroom. He said nothing to his mother who was the only one there. This kind of entrance had become standard when his father was not around. He had tried it a couple of times when his father was home and got hit each time. "That is no way to come into this house. You say hello," his father would say. Sometimes when his father came home late, smelling, he would say this to himself, and say hello to the chair and the sofa, but not to his mother. They would say nothing to each other. Frankie did not even want to say this much to his parents, but neither did he want to get hit. His mother would say nothing to his father. He was safe. He slammed the bedroom door. It wasn't her fault—but it sure wasn't his, either.

The machine clicked.

Frankie beat up the machine as long and as hard as he could. Longer than hours. The machine's sobbing had stopped. The messages on the screen had long since disappeared. Frankie dropped onto his bed, exhausted. He could hear his mother crying quietly in the next room. She was always crying, and thought she could not be heard. But it was always the only noise when the clock stopped, and the clock always stopped.

Frankie was an only child. His mother had become very ill at his birth and could have no more children. But, being a good Catholic, she tried again and came very near the sounds of death the second time around. This is what she said to everyone. No chance to be like other families. No chance to live like them. No chance for anything, not even a new clock. Because of this, even, they lived in the smallest of the apartments, the one on the end that looked like it had been accidental. Things were always quiet in Frankie's house. Sometimes there were the two noises only, sometimes the one. The clock. His mother. Both of them crazy. But inside, inside him, there were also noises, too many sometimes to hold in his head, even with his hands pressing.

He listened to them now. He never could be like the others, he knew, because of the noises. His link to the boys, Frankie's big chance of letting the noises leak out, was now broken. They were laughing at him. He had tried too hard to have brothers, even sisters, and now they were picking on him. Everyone was picking on him, he knew it. The Lopers. Mr. Johnson, his father, the teacher who had turned him in to the principal. His mother. He always.got caught. They had all been picking on him for a long time now. It was as if they had all decided to beat him up, together, and he couldn't fight back. They held him, sat on his chest, on his stomach. He couldn't laugh it off, not any more. Everything was loud. The machine clicked.

Frankie stood up, fists clenched to start again. He touched the machine.

Ha ha ha ho ho hee ha ho hee ha ha

Frankie stood still. The laughing continued. The ritual had begun. He did nothing. The laughing slowed. He stepped in front of it again. He kicked it, hearing the sort-of thud just above the last of the laughter. The sobbing began. The same messages kept rowing back and forth across the screen. Frankie touched the leathery bag. The light sobbing continued, but he wasn't listening now to that noise. He began stroking the bag, looking for the seam without thinking about it. They would not let him have a dog in the development. Not even a dog. He had no one. He saw some scuff marks where he had kicked the machine. The screen still had its message.

"I'm sorry," whispered Frankie. There was no response from the machine. He walked back to his bed, falling on it, not even trying to stop himself. He had been picking on the machine as everyone had been picking on him. He had kicked it and beat it up and it had cried. Frankie thought about crying, too. Inside. All the noises. Sometimes they had a sound. But he decided that he was too big really to cry. At least he had that over the machine. He had that.

Frankie stayed on the bed for a long while, thinking about this thing in front of him. It was like him. A lot. The machine did nothing to get beat up for. It was not Frankie's fault that he had gotten caught. Or that Mr. Johnson came over every day. Or that he lived where he did. Or that he wasn't big enough to beat up any of the other guys. Or the noises in the house. Inside him, even. It wasn't.

Frankie walked over to the machine, touched it, then waited. It clicked.

Ha ha ha ho ho hee ha ho hee ha ha

He let the machine laugh. He would not beat it up. Just like that. And he would not let himself get beat up anymore, there would be a way. Or get caught, either. He would fight back. He could become a kind of partner with this machine. So. Neither one would be picked on anymore. They could both laugh together. Nobody would pick on it, not this fat cousin. He stroked the bag again and the laughter quieted. He had learned. This intruder was a good thing after all. This machine, this friend. This brother, maybe.

Frankie sat back on the bed and leaned with both his elbows. He decided he would get Mr. Johnson first.

Johnny Ray

Let me tell you that when any of the boys used to talk to him they would call him HEY Johnny RAY just to watch his cheeks turn red, nice big fat ones, and of course he was always the boy who blushed so red he was nothing but clown cheeks. I guess he came into his own sometime around about junior high school when the story was going around about his sister Patsy. Now Patsy was a story in herself, but she went off to school somewhere and nobody knew exactly where that was, but then, nobody exactly cared, either. She had some sort of bladder infection or something and one day she just kinda let loose in class and pretty soon there was a regular old Mississippi—remember the old bouncing ball cartoon that showed you how to spell that? Well there was a regular old Mis-sis-sippi shooting right off one of the legs of her desk. Of course everybody started laughing and Mrs. Snow got pretty angry and sent everyone out of the room. I say angry cause Mrs. Snow was the one in our school who always used to say that only dogs got mad. Anyway, it was too late to keep anybody from knowing what happened cause kids are pretty quick when something exciting is going on.

I guess it was just after that when Patsy didn't come back to school anymore. I suppose we were pretty mean to Patsy, school kids are some-times, but we didn't try to be, not on purpose. We just wanted to see what was going on, and what was going on was mighty funny. Us Mexican kids, who were in the majority then, started laughing in Spanish and the rest laughed just as hard in what I guess you'd call English. Funny is funny, I guess. That's another thing about Johnny Ray and his family. They just seemed misplaced. Everyone round these parts was Mexican save his family and maybe one or two other missionary families. We all just sort of fit in and got to gettin along except those Tisons. They just kinda stuck out like books in a house. They were, well I don't know for sure, Seventh Day Adventists or somesuch and were just too pushy for the Mexicans, so them Tisons sort of had to take to being ignored, a lot, even with all the help my papa and the rest try to give 'em. I don't suppose they ever changed, though, just moved around from place to place, to this day I'd guess.

Well, suppose it was because I lived next to him that Johnny Ray and me sort of got thrown together by fate or something. Those Tisons came from the missionary families who kinda treated us Mexicans different, like we had to be changed or something, like we didn't do stuff right, and this is probably why we treated them different. Of course our families still got along, talking and all that, but it was different. Johnny Ray's father always had that big left eye on you no matter what you was saying. Me and Johnny Ray, though, we got to know each other pretty well when his father wasn't around. After all, we were the last ones to get off the school bus. Maybe we got to know each other too well for my liking. I mean, you just *knew* Johnny Ray was gonna grow up to be just like his father. Not yet, but he would. He wouldn't get no smarter or anything than his father, he would just still be a missionary. One that did exactly the same stuff. I guess he was just like my father, too, and the rest of the missionaries and the rest of the Mexicans when they were all small. I hate to talk about my father that way, comparing him to Johnny Ray and all, but it's probably pretty true. I don't want you to think I'm saying I thought us Mexicans were all that much better cause I didn't, not all the time. But I did always figger there had to be some kinda island in the middle, you know what I mean? Like a playground we could all get dirty in. Nobody else seemed to, not even Johnny Ray when we talked about it. That's why I thought he'd grow up just like his papa and mine. Fathers said funny things about other fathers.

Now I used to go over to Johnny Ray's a lot cause I figgered there was hope for everybody. But it seemed like every time I got there he was making bread. That isn't so bad except you just *knew* he was a guy who would make bread even though he wasn't sissy or anything like that as far as I could tell. I guess I don't blame him though. I mean those Tisons didn't have no TV or anything. Johnny Ray used to read for fun, if you can imagine that. I guess if I was having fun like that I would consider giving it up to make bread, too, or baskets or something. I mean I probably would have even taken up something like sewing, you know what I mean? It wasn't till later I found out Johnny Ray sewed, too. I figger I was just always afraid to ask him cause I was afraid for the worst. I could of bet on it, though, and I would of except that I don't think none of the guys would of taken the bet.

Well, I thought I knew Johnny Ray pretty well by this time, both personal and story-wise. I even knew the latest story, something about his picking his nose then sticking his finger in his mouth. Some even said he used to swallow. One day we even organized, and took turns watching all day. I never said nothing, either, to Johnny Ray about these stories, and I guess that's just as well. I think it's better that he didn't know. And besides, I was kinda afraid of the worst after I found out about his sewing.

By this time I had found out lots of things about Johnny Ray which is why I still remember him and why probably everybody else does too. You could likely describe almost everything about him without even knowing him. I mean stuff like that he always wore glasses with black rims and had them since I think second grade. And he always wore green jeans. And he always read science-fiction, and probably believed it. And his father always read science-fiction, and probably believed it. And his father always gave him haircuts with his mother helping out like a back seat driver even though he had short hair to begin with. And he always brought one of those big can openers to school in his sack lunch so that he had to carry it around with him the rest of the day. He always stuck it in the same pocket as his lunch bag, which he always folded and saved. I think in one school year he probably didn't use more than two bags. And he always wore a big watch with a worn black band. And he always did his homework even if he didn't always do it well. He wasn't real smart all the time but he tried real hard. And his bread. You can't help mentioning his bread every time you talk about Johnny Ray. I guess the list could go on forever, but you get the idea. I think you could know him real well without really knowing him. Thing is, I did know him.

Now like I said, nobody hardly talked to Johnny Ray, just about him. I guess in this he was a little bit lucky cause he never had to worry about getting beat up or anything, like I did. Everybody just plain left him alone. It was kinda magic sometimes, I think, and that's how come I used to hang around him a lot of the time.

Of course it was because of all this that I guess I shouldn't have been surprised at what happened that day in class, but I was. It was *El Día del Vaquero*, cowboy day, you know, and everybody was supposed to come to school dressed up like a cowboy or Indian. It was real popular in this town cause everybody seemed to come from a ranch sometime along the way and they enjoyed dressing up. Cap guns and stuff like that were real popular, too. The school held a special assembly in the morning— remember assemblies?—just for skits and things and then they gave us a two-hour lunch period, and to top that off we got to leave school early. You can imagine. It was a real perfect holiday.

Well, it was that day in school and everybody came dressed up pretty good. Some of the richer kids even came with real rawhide chaps and everybody was making a real fuss over them, and there were lots of

49

Indians with real stuff, and Mexican in-between things. Then the school bus came, and of course, Johnny Ray rode the school bus. I did, too, but that's different. You just could of guessed he did. Johnny Ray also came dressed as if this was any other day. He had his green jeans on which was all right, but he also had on his white shirt—more or less white—, his black surplus shoes, his red socks, and his watch. Now Johnny Ray was *really* out of place. Neon, if you know what I mean.

Now you know of course this was no big crime or nothing like that but Johnny Ray knew as well as any other person in that school what the seniors did at lunch time if you didn't have at least three western things on. And those seniors, let me give you a clue, weren't above anything or anybody. I must of had on ten or twenty things just to be absolutely sure. Of course that would be at lunch time, so Johnny Ray could get along okay until at least eleven-thirty, which is when they started.

Exactly what it was these seniors did every year was, first of all, build a jail out of plywood and put it up where everybody could see it for about two days before the festivities. Then on the *Día del Vaquero* they would come around to all the classes at about eleven and look for people who weren't dressed up. Then they'd put a rope around whoever wasn't and haul them off to jail. Now these people would have to stay in jail until twelve-thirty or so when they could pay a fifty-cent fine and get out. But, whoever didn't want to pay the fine got taken in a pick-up about five miles out of town and had to walk back. It was all done in fun and mostly nobody got mad or nothing, just mostly drunk though the principal would never say so. This had been going on for just about as long as the school had been built, which was a considerable piece of time.

So, like I said, Johnny Ray could get by till then, eleven or eleven-thirty, and he did. Nobody said nothing to him and he didn't say anything to anybody about it, except me cause I asked him. I was kinda curious and I had him for American history or somesuch at ten so I went up to him and I asked him if he knew what he was in for and he said he didn't care. Then I asked him why he didn't dress up cause I knew he had enough cowboy-looking clothes to pass, or I could even lend him some, and he said he just didn't want to, that's all. I figgered I had learned enough, which really wasn't nothing but it was enough considering it was Johnny Ray I had been talking to. I was just mighty glad I had dressed up enough. Mighty glad.

Everybody else was having a grand time of it shooting cap guns and showing off and of course nobody was paying much attention to school work. It was probably one of the best school days we had that year, even with what happened later.

At about eleven-fifteen or so, we could hear the vigilante posse of seniors roping and tying up a few kids who weren't dressed up. Most of them were juniors and probably didn't dress up on purpose. They were hollering and carrying on so much we had a hard time hearing the teacher, not that anybody was straining. It wouldn't be long before they got to our class. Johnny Ray was the only one who was gonna get carried off. We were all pretty anxious cause it was gonna be mighty funny to see Johnny Ray turn red and get carried off and all.

Well, when they finally did get to our room, about five of those seniors jangled in all dressed up so there wasn't a lick of regular person in them. They were all dressed up as Mexican *vaqueros,* and a couple of them reminded me of the pictures I had seen of Zapata when he had those two gun belts wrapped around his chest and looked hard tough. They was making all kinds of fuss and finally one of them stands up front and yells out, "We have come for anybody not dressed up like a *vaquero!*" You could tell right off by the way he said *vaquero* that he was one of us. It was a funny thing, but it sounded just like it should and just like none of those missionaries ever could say it no matter how long they tried. The teacher sat back and enjoyed the scene pretty much. Miss James was all right. Now all these seniors started to shooting off their cap guns and rifles and started to looking around. Of course, they all headed for Johnny Ray just about right off but he didn't look up. It was about this time that everything seemed to sort of slow down like it was taking years or something. You ever been in an accident? Well it always happens right before important things and so that was right off a sign of what was to come.

When those five seniors got to Johnny Ray it was like setting off a firecracker before you're ready and they was all too close. I swear I never seen nothing like it and I never thought Johnny Ray would be the one to show me. It was TV, pure and simple. Of course Johnny Ray couldn't have known that, but he was a natural. Johnny Ray got the hand of the first guy who touched him and threw it as if he was throwing a football. The guy nearly twirled around right where he was standing. Then Johnny Ray got his whole big notebook, that gray-blue kind, you know? and threw it the length of the room. I swear it was a pretty sight when all the papers flew out all over the place and it hit a desk right up in front. It nearly caught the boy sitting there right square in his open mouth, the kind of open mouths fathers always say are gonna catch flies. Now all this was happening while Johnny Ray was still sitting down.

By this time all the seniors had backed off quite a piece and I think two of them were hiding in the big closet back there. Anyway, it gave

Johnny Ray room to stand up, and jeez he was in such a hurry to stand up that he brought his desk with him so it fell over and all his books kinda slid down the aisle. Now by this time, Miss James, who was usually all right like I said, was sorta screaming her head off and everybody else was just watching and talking as if this was Saturday morning at the movies or something. Better, even. Nobody was getting up to go to the bathroom.

Now everybody, by this time, had noticed something kinda queer about the whole situation and that was that Johnny Ray wasn't saying nothing like you'd probably expect. I mean he was as red in the face as I'd ever seen him and his eyes were streaming water down his round cheeks so they was dripping but he wasn't saying nothing, just holding his breath I think. Of course everybody else pretty much made up for it cause they were all jabbering and Miss James was still yelling louder and louder so she could be heard, "Johnny Ray! Johnny Ray Tison you stop that this instant! Johnny Ray you listen to me and stop that! Johnny Ray!"

It didn't do much good. By this time he had stood up and had kicked his desk over to the window and had picked up a book and threw it at one of the seniors. Now Miss James came marching as mad as gray cats down the aisle and she grabbed that Johnny Ray by the arm which was lucky cause she couldn't get hit but Johnny Ray kicked her instead. Johnny Ray still had nothing to say but he was crying and all red now like his head was gonna bust open like a stepped-on tomato. "Johnny Ray, I'm taking you straight to the principal's office!" Johnny Ray had calmed down a little by the time she said this, since all the seniors had got out of this town after one got kicked. Miss James stomped out with Johnny Ray and we were all left just watching.

Well we had an awful lot of talking and comparing to do so you can imagine the state the classroom was in by now. I swear five languages was being spoken all at once and I could understand all of them. Of course it wasn't too long before another teacher came in and dismissed the class, which made the whole thing even better cause it was only twenty till twelve and so we felt kinda special after all this happening.

I guess you can still hear this story lots of different ways like that Johnny Ray really did hit somebody with his notebook or that when he kicked Miss James there was blood spilling out all over the place but I don't remember it that way. Still, this is my favorite story about him, good ole Johnny Ray. I heard later that he didn't get into too much trouble or anything cause those seniors didn't really have any right or anything to take him out if he didn't want to go, and I guess he showed that all right. His folks came down to the principal's office and there was a pretty big fuss and everything, but like I said, he didn't get into too much trouble. Of course he didn't talk to nobody again, not even me. And that was his last year at that school, too. I guess he went away to where his sister Patsy was but nobody cared enough to find out for sure. It was sorta like when Patsy left, I think. Come to think of it, that might've been the year his whole family moved away but I can't remember if it was that way for sure.

Now I gotta say to this day, and I hate to admit it, but his bread was awful good to taste. I just kinda wish now I had asked him how to make it before he left. Now I mean I wouldn't have took up sewing or anything like that, but I just gotta say that his bread was probably, no, it was the best I ever tasted when that honey got to dripping down the sides and I had a little butter, real stuff. Yeah, good old Johnny Ray. He made the butter too, and had bees.

The Way Spaghetti Feels

She was more normal, more special than red balloons. Everyone told her that. They all had different names for it, different ways of describing her, but it all came down to balloons. Red ones. She had braces, a permanent, a couple of pairs of the right jeans, she was growing, not too much, she was popular, she could sing, she was Mexican, she could dance the Mexican dances everyone always wanted to see, she had only a few *things* on her face, no really bad pimples. Everything normal. Everything bright. Balloons. Red. But now her secret made her feel as though she were going to break.

Mari sat on her bed and tied her blue Nikes. The Greek goddess of winged victory, like that statue in the Literature book. That teacher who came for a week told her. She thought maybe she could run faster, but told only her father. Everyone else would have laughed at her, and she told him so. But he said he understood, and she believed it. When he was little he had a pair of something called *P.F. Flyers,* and when he wore them he could jump, *SAS!* higher than the telephone poles. Really. Mari laughed at him instead.

Today was Saturday, and for the first time in a long while she didn't have anything to get done. Not anything that anybody knew about, anyway. Ballet was cancelled. She was glad, yes yes, because she wouldn't have been able to go today, and how would she have explained that. She loved ballet, and had pictures balanced all over her walls. No, today she didn't have anything to do—except break. Burst! She might break, Pssst! just like that, and nobody would ever know where she was because she'd be in a thousand pieces. She pulled her shoestring tight, like the string on a balloon. She couldn't even tell her father. Her secret was even too big for that. Bigger than her own head, that's what it felt like, so it hurt, but she couldn't tell, not anyone.

"Maricela!" She heard her mother call. Mari looked in her mirror and then went out. She would have to act normal, like always. But how could she, she thought. They would know. They always knew. Her father, especially.

"Yes, what." Good, thought Mari, he wasn't here. She could fool her mother.

"Where are you going today?" Her mother didn't look up from the breakfast she was making. It was *chorizo,* and Mari thought it smelled wonderful. If only she could tell just her mother. It must have smelled wonderful all her life, but she never paid as much attention to the smell as now. How could she not have paid attention to it all this time. Her head kept pretending to think about the food, but she was really just wishing she could have a second chance.

"Oh, what? What do you want?" Mari tried to cover up. She sat at the table and her mother served her.

"We need some tortillas. Flour ones. Your father went, you know, to play the pool, and he won't get to the *tortillería* in time. I want you to get some hot ones. They should be ready by now. I told them to save me two dozens."

"Okay. I need the money." This would work out. The factory for tortillas was near where she had to go. If things worked out, well then great, she'd have the tortillas and everything would be fine. It would be the second chance, the smell of *chorizo.* And if things didn't work out, well, at least they would see that she had bought the tortillas. That she had done something good. That she didn't mean to do anything wrong. Really.

"They'll charge them. I told la Mrs. Sandoval already that you'd come for them."

"Okay." She finished her breakfast, and went to the bathroom to brush her teeth. Maybe this would be the last time. She looked in the mirror at the face with the toothbrush in its mouth, a bristle caught in the braces as always. Stupid. Maybe nobody would miss her. A hand in the mirror pulled at the toothbrush. Or maybe they would all come looking, like a posse, like in the movies, because they did miss her. Soon enough, she thought, she would know.

It had been going on for almost a year. Even through the winter. And she couldn't tell anybody, not her best friends, not her parents, not her dog. That was the first rule. Well, it was a rule in the beginning, but now she just couldn't. It didn't have to be a rule anymore. It was like taking a shower in gym class. First she didn't want to, it was too embarrassing, but now it made sense. She didn't want to smell, not even once. People got teased for that. And other stuff, even worse.

It was a secret. Exactly that. But a real one, not the fake kind where everybody knows. The kind that's supposed to be a real secret but where you wouldn't be a real friend if you didn't tell the other girls you did stuff with. These are the fun kind, really, because everybody can talk about them, and they make everybody breathe faster because nobody can believe it, whatever it is. That kind of secret. Fake. Not a bad fake, just fake.

Like periods. Nobody could decide if this was a real secret or not. When it came, Mari thought, she wanted to tell everyone because she was happy—finally, God. But how could she tell her father? And she *certainly* could not bring it up in class, like birthdays, or let the boys know. Stupids. Yet it was the first thing she told the other girls. And her mother. She told her friends first, but then had to tell her mother real fast because she wasn't sure what to do. She had talked about it with the girls, of course, and she wasn't the first, but they didn't really know what to do either. Even the ones who had it already. The stuff they said sounded gross. But when she told her mother, it was all true. They all talked about the idea of it, and they had seen the movies and things at school, but when the real day came, none of that counted. It was great and it was gross, for awhile. The fake kind of secret.

But it had a real secret part, too. That's the part you can't talk about. Like earlier in eighth grade, in Mrs. Lipscomb's social studies class. She had already started having periods, so it wasn't real shocking when it happened, but the whole thing was still fairly new. Some girls talked about it. She knew other people, too, outside of her friends, had been having periods because starting in seventh grade when someone had a period in PE she just said "M" and didn't have to shower. Mari did anyway, now, but you didn't have to. You said it at roll call, and so everybody heard. It was probably "M" for menstruation, but nobody ever said, not even the gym teacher, and no one asked. You pretended it didn't even almost exist and except with your friends you never asked anybody about the whole thing.

Two things happened in Mrs. Lipscomb's class to show why you didn't ever talk about it. Even, sometimes, with friends. Mari had homeroom, then a break, then social studies, all in the same room after lunch. Her homeroom class had been meeting and everyone got up for the break and to go to other classes. Mari was one of the last to begin standing. Mrs. Lipscomb was standing in the back of the room and told Mari to sit back down please, that she wanted to speak to her. Everybody left and she came over to Mari. She told her that she had stained her dress.

Mari figured that Mrs. Lipscomb maybe thought this was her first period, but it wasn't and so Mari wasn't too shocked by the news about, well, blood. It was just hard to take care of it at first, to know what was going to happen, how much. All that. But Mari was glad that Mrs. Lipscomb thought this was her first time because she took care of her. Mrs. Lipscomb was very gentle with Mari, even though she was a real tough teacher and all the students were kind of afraid of her. She demanded a lot of her pupils, she always said, and didn't always seem very nice. But she was real sweet to Mari—that's the word she thought of later, sweet. Mari wasn't afraid of her exactly, but this was too nice almost. That was scary. "Honey," she called her. Sweet names. This must be serious. She said they were going to the nurse's office because of her dress, the stain. But she shouldn't worry, this was all normal—all things that Mari had heard before. But Mari wasn't nervous—just real embarrassed that Mrs. Lipscomb, or anybody, had seen her. But she had told Mari to sit down in class early enough so that no one else had seen her, she said, even though Mari didn't ask. Just Mrs. Lipscomb—that really wasn't so bad. Mari would never forget her. And she said then that she was going to walk behind Mari to the nurse's office, and they'd find or do something, and all that stuff. So they went, and Mrs. Lipscomb did walk behind like she said so no one would look. There wasn't anyone out in the hall, really, but Mari was glad. They washed out her dress in the nurse's office. The back of it, anyway. The nurse called her "honey" too. It wasn't really terrible or anything, they said. Mari said so, too, so they wouldn't feel bad, but she didn't believe it. The nurse gave her a clean pad and Mari went back to class after her dress had dried. It didn't take long and she wasn't late. No one knew, not even her friends. Mari felt different about Mrs. Lipscomb. Something good. A secret. About something bad. A real secret is what it was. She didn't tell anyone. That kind of secret.

But a couple of months later, and confident that she wasn't staining her dress anymore because now she was super careful and could judge what would happen to her better, Mari was sitting in class. She must not have had the real hang of it, yet. She wouldn't have known this until she got home, and even wouldn't have worried too much about having a period because she was confident now, except....

In Mrs. Lipscomb's class again, after social studies this time, when everyone was leaving, there were these two guys. The class was U-shaped, and they sat across from her. She must have sat, she supposed, some way so that they could see. Of all the days to wear a dress. Jorge and Ruben. They were both Mexican, too, but kind of punky guys, tough. Not mean, really, just tough. The kind that told jokes while the teacher was trying to do something. Forgot their homework and shrugged their shoulders. That kind of stuff. Even though they were Mexican, their names were pronounced American. Jorge was "George," and Rubén was Ruben. Jorge was great big and fat and funny. Ruben was real skinny, and they always hung around together. They sat together in class, of course. And, she guessed, they really were funny. Jorge was. Ruben just kind of laughed. Jorge threw basketballs made of wadded paper as Ruben announced the new Dr. J.

As everyone was leaving the class, these two were giggling and talking to each other, but loud enough so Mari could hear. She wasn't sure if they really meant for her to hear, but they said something about uhhh, how terrible, how disgusting—Mari couldn't remember the words—but saying something about what they had seen. It might have been Spanish. They talked in Spanish a lot, and knew she understood. They must have been direct, though. She remembered that she went straight to the bathroom after it happened, this time without even Mrs. Lipscomb. She could hear them still—oooohhh, bloody *calzones*—that's what they probably said. Mari understood. Whether they said real words or not, just from their faces she understood.

Her first thought was to rush out.

Her second was that they were going to go out and tell all their friends. They would do that.

She went to the bathroom. It did happen, the stain. She changed, which was all she could do. She didn't need any help this time—but she sure wished it had been Mrs. Lipscomb again, and not.... There was one more class. She went because she had to—she was too good a student, and would be missed. She couldn't get away with anything. She went to class and when she sat down she lifted up her dress so she wouldn't sit on it, just in case anything happened again. She felt real nervous—not as before a test. Real nervous. She sat through class. Right after class she usually went to her locker and waited for her friends because she always walked home with them. But after this class she was so embarrassed because she knew these guys, who walked in the same general direction with other guys—sometimes throwing rocks at the girls and stuff— would be there, and she didn't want to see anyone. So she waited, and walked home alone.

The next day she really didn't want to go back to school. She was sure they would have told everyone—they weren't like Mrs. Lipscomb. All their guy friends. So they could all have a laugh. She thought she could be sick, maybe. It made her face turn red just to think of what had happened. This was new, and somehow sexual, boys seeing. She knew it was something she was going to have to deal with. Mari knew once you had a period you could have a baby. That's why it was embarrassing. She wasn't brought up so that it was just a bodily function, this period thing, normal and natural and you shouldn't be ashamed of it. You were very weird about it—well, not weird, but it wasn't something to talk about, not on and on with strangers. And if you did talk, it was only to girls. Mothers, sometimes, about parts. Not this. And now *they* knew. And she couldn't go tell them not to tell. She couldn't talk to them at all. She felt as if she had eaten a huge dinner, a Thanksgiving one, but instead of food it was embarrassment. Stuffed into her. That feeling.

She did go to school. She didn't have a reason not to go, not one that she could tell, and her mother would have been very suspicious if she just stayed home. And she'd have to go to school sometime. And her mother would tell her father. Her father. So she went and she did her best to avoid the two guys. Jorge and Ruben were part of a group of guys that hung out together before school, too, standing by the fence that everyone had to go through to get to school. Saying things, pulling hair. Stuff.

Mari remembered thinking that when she got to school they'd be there and she was sure everybody would know. At first she couldn't face them. But they never did mention it again. Getting through the first day was a relief, but she suspected that they told—they were the type that called people names, four-eyes, tin mouth. But maybe not. All their friends were kind of loud, and they would have used *it* for a laugh. But maybe Jorge and Ruben had secrets, too. They were jerks anyway.

Now this wasn't fake, she thought as she finished breakfast, not this secret. Like the period stuff when they saw. This one she couldn't tell anyone, either. She might have in the beginning, because everything was so silly, but she didn't because no one was around, and then it was too late. Like in those movies where someone is found with a dead body or something, but they didn't do it, they were just there for some stupid reason but going to jail is almost easier because the explanation, the real one, sounds so ridiculous and takes about eight years to make it make sense.

She thought as she walked, slowly, out of her house toward the *tortillería*. The whole thing began during Easter vacation the year before. As easy as anything, the last day of school, back when everything seemed so simple—no periods, no homework that took more than five minutes, lots of dancing, no stupid boys. It was vacation and Mari felt great walking home. She had to bring home only two books and she was eating a chocolate Easter egg that she had gotten at her class party. The party was great and nobody had really done any work in the morning. Days before holidays were like that. They were the real holidays, the real fun days. That was always more fun than the real stuff that had to be done on Easter itself, or Christmas. Having a big party with all her friends was very different from sitting around at her grandmother's house where she was supposed to look pretty in a new dress. Everybody was going to try and make her smile so they could tease her about her braces. She wouldn't. She decided this with the last bite of her candy egg. Chomp. Just like that.

Her path home was a good ways, about a mile. Sometimes her mother would give her a ride if she asked, but she liked the walk. There was a long way and a short way, and her mother always told her to get home as fast as she could. But, thought Mari, she was older now, not a kid as before, and she could take the long way if she wanted. This walk was a thousand times prettier, besides — even if it did smell so much.

Most of the long way went next to a cow pasture that had about six million Black Angus cows. Mari always stopped and looked. It reminded her of something African, like the book they had in her classroom. The cows were black, the ground was brown — not always dirt — and the straw was straw-color. All the African pictures looked like that. It made her feel as if she were traveling when she squinted her eyes and pretended. Everything got fuzzy, as in a dream. As if she were there, wherever "there" was.

And sometimes the cows knew her. Well, she thought so. She picked one out as her favorite and looked everyday to see it, but she wasn't sure it was the same one always. Ogie-Tooga. It was the only thing she could think of that sounded African. Well, she really didn't even know what African sounded like, so this was close enough. For her cow dream anyway. When she first used to come by this pasture she never paid any real attention to anything, but now things were different. She had a friend who had a sheep and had to sell it, but didn't want to after she had raised it and everything. Petunia. That was the sheep. And what she said about the sheep made Mari think about the cows. Nobody pays attention to the cows. One cow gets all the ooh's and ahh's and love that exists in the universe, but hundreds.... Just like people, thought Mari. She had seen pictures of people in Africa, but she didn't know anybody. It was hard to feel sorry for them. Maybe, with Ogie-Tooga, well it made her conscience feel better. She tried to explain it to the priest during confession, but he didn't get it. So she didn't talk to anybody about the cows anymore. Ogie-Tooga was all hers. A real secret. She knew the other girls would just laugh if she tried to explain, like the priest did. So this was the secret. Not a fake-o.

But she was wrong. Even now, she thought, the cow secret was pretty silly. Compared, of course, to the real thing, which happened next.

It was a cool day. Cold, probably, but Mari felt so good it was only cool. Before she had started from school she knew this was a long path day. It wasn't much of a choice even though the short way, aside from being shorter, smelled better. Right where she had to make her choice between the two ways was the *tortillería*. Going that way she would be followed by the smell of the freshly made tortillas, one of her favorite smells in the world. The other way she would have to smell cows, but that was okay with Mari today. Sometimes a smell is a smell, and any smell just means you're alive. Like when you smell a skunk—you certainly know you're alive.

She chose the long way, and as she walked along the narrow road and barbed wire fence that marked the pasture she looked right away for Ogie. Usually this made the time pass faster because, by the time she found the cow, or the one she thought was Ogie this time, she was practically at the end of the field.

Today she spotted Ogie almost right away. There was a string around her neck with a paper attached. At least it looked like that. And she was standing by the fence just up ahead. Mari always stopped and talked for a while, but something was different today. She reached the cow, and it didn't move.

"There, Ogie. There now, don't be scared. Ogie-Tooga. Yes it's just me." She looked at the cow, who looked back at her. Mari wondered what Ogie must think about the same things she said over and over and over. There there and don't be scared. But what else do you say to a cow.

It was a note. Or really, it was a pouch made from paper with a note sticking out of it, tied by some regular string. Mari reached for it, but the cow moved away. All the other cows were looking now. The "moo's" sounded more like "who's" that. Animals start to talk like that sometimes.

A barbed wire fence separated them. Mari wished she still had some of her chocolate egg, but no no no, she had to go and be a little pig. "Come here, come on Ogie. Ohh, little fatso Og, come here baby." Did she say little? Mari wondered if cows knew about lying. About 32 clowns could fit into Ogie, like the ones that fit in that car at the circus.

Ogie did not come.

Mari put her stuff on the ground. A note is a note, after all, whether it's being handed to you across a desk or whether it's on a cow's fat neck. She had no idea what it could say, or if it was even a real note. But that made it better.

Just as if she were a kid, she went where there was a pole in the fence, and put one foot on the wire, then the other foot on the next wire, and up and up, then a jump. Her dress went up like a parachute, but it was okay. There weren't any boys here, only cows. Do cows care, she wondered, about seeing? "Mooo." "Oooo." They sounded exactly like the boys. "Cut it out, caca-heads!"

"Oh, but not you Ogie. Don't be scared. Come on, I won't hurt you." The cow was considering which way to run. "Come on, I don't want you in my hamburger. It's okay." She reached out, very slowly. The cow smelled her. What nerve, thought Mari, smelling *her*.

It was okay. Mari patted her head. She pulled out the note, and unfolded.

Hi. Is anyone out there? Put the answer back on the cow.

What is this, thought Mari, how stupid.

Maybe. But okay. It was like a message in a bottle. That wasn't so bad. Besides, she had gone this far. This was work. She didn't really think it would be a note, not really, but she wished it would be. Sort of. And here it was, in her hand. Now what. That's the problem when you wish for stuff and then get it.

She went back to the fence, kneeled down, and reached through to her stuff to get a pen. She wrote back, on the same piece of paper:

Hi back. Yes, somebody's out here.

She refolded and managed to get it back into the pouch on Ogie. She guessed this was Ogie, anyway. It must have been—and someone else could tell she was a special cow, too. Ha!

And that's how everything began. Just like that. "Hi back."

But that wasn't the end. No no no.

The second note was on the same piece of paper. She had made a special trip back on Monday, even though it was vacation. Not that there was supposed to be a second note or anything, but....

ALRIGHT! Are you still there? Put the answer back on the cow.

It should have been two words, thought Mari, "all right." She was a good student. How stupid. "Are you still there" and "put the answer back on the cow." What was she going to do with it. What did he think—wait, she stopped. Was it a boy or a girl? She couldn't tell by the writing. But it was somebody left handed—you could tell—and people's writing looks a lot more the same if they're left handed. She wrote back.

Yes, I'm still here. Who are you?

And she put the note back on the cow. It was still the same piece of paper. There wasn't much room left on it. A boy or a girl. This had to be a boy. Only they would do this. Stupids. She hoped for a boy, anyway. It sounded like a boy. Who wanted to write to a girl, thought Mari. This way, anyway.

She couldn't come the next day, or the day after, or the day after that. Relatives had come to visit from Mexico, from Guaymas, and her cousin, also named Maricela, stayed with her the whole time. This was okay, but she was younger. A year. She thought about telling her, but she couldn't. The notes were for Mari. They did walk by the cows, though. Her cousin thought the pasture smelled, *"fui,"* but Mari only laughed. Not really at her cousin, but because she could see a note on Ogie. It was there, and it was a new piece of paper, she could tell. Her cousin's visits were always a lot of fun, but this time she was driving Mari crazy. Later she confessed that she wished for her cousin to go home, and the priest had laughed at her again. She wished he would stop laughing at the important things.

Besides, she couldn't have explained to Maricela, her cousin, even if she had wanted to. Even though they had the same name, they weren't the same. Not as they used to be. They could both dance and stuff, but talking to her was hard now. They used to have kind of their own language, all mixed up with English and Spanish and invented words, but it didn't work the same now. Neither one knew as many words to speak to each other as they used to. Her cousin's Spanish was very good, and Mari's English was very good, too. She had won awards, and her parents were proud. They let her show them things in English, explain stuff, but they didn't really show her the other way around, in Spanish. Mari noticed for the first time.

But finally her cousin left, and Mari went first thing to look for the new note. This was getting exciting. Stupid, but okay.

You want to be friends? But it's gotta be a secret, okay? Put the answer back on the cow.

And underneath that, written later she could tell, was more.

Where are you?

So he, if this was a he, had missed her. But he still didn't say who he was. Very strange. Now she wanted to know more than ever. She wrote back.

I'm still here. I couldn't come. Okay, I want to be friends. It's a secret, though.

She put it back on the cow. She thought about waiting around to see if anyone came, but she had to get home. It was still vacation—which wasn't really vacation. Her parents had a thousand things for her to do. Parents are like that. They don't get it about vacations.

School started again on Monday. It was all different. For the first time, the first real time for a real reason, she wanted school to be over. Seeing everybody and talking was good, but hard. If this note-stuff was a real secret, she couldn't tell. Not anybody. But she didn't know if it was yet, so even though she wanted to tell all of her friends, she didn't. She could've, but then things would have been different. Everybody would have wanted to come with her after school, and then it wouldn't have been fun, not the same kind of fun. This wouldn't have been her secret anymore. It would have been everyone's. A fake-o. No. This was different.

After school she didn't wait around for anyone or anything. She practically ran home. The way she used to run when she was smaller and had gotten a new bike, or the skates. She couldn't wait. But maybe she should've. This time she slipped. Right onto the ground in her dress as she jumped over the fence. Her blue dress wasn't blue anymore. *Really* wasn't blue. Cow pastures sometimes aren't kind. They're like cactus. Sometimes they get you. She'd have some explaining to do—more, even, than with the period stuff, because this didn't make sense—but it didn't matter. She got the note. It was getting easier—she brought sugar with her now. Ogie had learned.

Okay, friend. It's a deal. Secret. So don't leave the notes anymore—use a clean piece of paper in case somebody finds out. Put the answer back on the cow.

She got a clean piece of paper. That made sense. But there was something she had to say.

Okay, friend. Listen, you don't have to keep telling me to put the answer back on the cow, okay? How are you?

64

And so things went on. It was lucky, thought Mari the very next time, that he—it had to be a he—had said to keep using a different piece of paper each time. When she got there next to look for the note, Ogie didn't have one. But not because it wasn't written. Somebody, the owner probably, had found it. But the messages were so involved now, answers where you had to know the question, that the note must not have made any sense. The note, and the pouch and the string, had been thrown on the ground. But on a ground that is mostly brown, the white of the paper stood out. Mari got her note.

And the weeks and weeks and weeks went on. They talked about all sorts of stuff—and it was a boy, she had finally asked. Sometimes they didn't answer right away, but there was always a reason. And Mari never told, and he never told. That's what he said, anyway, and she believed him. It was good.

For a long time she talked about dancing, about when she signed up for ballet, and he talked about baseball, and that he got a uniform. Regular stuff. And always without names. They agreed that they wouldn't use any names so the other could guess, maybe, who they were and so only one would know. That wouldn't be fair. So no names.

But one day the regular stuff changed. Mostly because Mari's regular life changed. It was when she got her period. Or really, a couple of days afterward. She had told her friends at school, and her mother. This was a kind-of secret, but the fake-o kind, and that's not as good. And the way she had talked about it so far, well, you don't really tell everything, thought Mari. So she decided to tell…,he didn't have a name. It just occurred to her. She wanted to tell him everything and he didn't even have a name. Og—like the cow. Not like all the cows, which sounded like all the boys, but like Ogie, the one cow. The one she liked.

She would tell him. A real secret, real stuff. No fake-o.

I got my period.

That's all, just like that. It felt good. It made her breathe faster. Would he tell her if he was a girl and had gotten a period? Nobody would. This was real-real stuff. She felt very nervous, but she was going to take a chance. Just not think about it, just do it. Fast. She ran. She let go of her note. She turned red, even though nobody was there. She ran, again. The red wouldn't go away. It felt great. Inside she was tight, but really because she wanted to laugh. Real laughs, not tiny ones. And real laughs hurt. It felt great.

She came right away the next day. This waiting stuff was the very hardest part, but it was faster than real letters. Still tough, though. Tough tough tough because she wanted to know *now*. It made her feel like going to the bathroom, and when she thought about it, the thinking made her toes go into a fist in her shoes. Nobody saw because the weather was still cool and she wasn't wearing sandals yet. In her Nikes. And her toes would get tight and tight and she wanted to laugh. Or go to the bathroom. Everything.

Period? Like a period period?

Boys! Sheesh.

Yes, like a period period.

Stupid, is what she wanted to say. But it was true—she and her friends had laughed a lot, too, whenever the teachers said stuff like that, stuff like where is your period, this sentence should have a period, and that's all I've got to say, period. The boys laughed, too.

Well, does it hurt? They showed us a movie in gym, but I didn't get it. It sounds terrible.

Their notes began to sound like a conversation then, like talking. For a while they went back and forth so fast this was almost like telegrams, thought Mari. Short, fast, just a couple of words. But it was as if those short notes weighed a thousand pounds.

Did it feel like going to the bathroom?

Everything about periods—he asked, and she told, and he laughed, a little, and she cried, a little, and they both laughed. In the notes. And then it happened, the day those boys saw her panties.

Mari didn't get a note next day after she told him. And when she did, it didn't say anything about the panties or the blood. It was something else. It was long. Not in words, but in what it said. She had been thinking only about herself.

I had a wet dream. You probably know what that is. They probably showed you a movie in gym class, like about periods. I guess. Well, I wet the sheets. It wasn't the first time, but I fixed it up the other times. This time my mother saw. This morning. I haven't been home yet. I don't want to go.

That's all, just like that. Wet dreams! It gave her that tight feeling inside. It was terrible—but she wanted to hear all about it. Gross! And all

66

the stuff the girls had laughed at in the movie, well, she remembered. Mari guessed it was the same kind of feeling, about not wanting to go home and his mother and all, as she had about the stain. She understood. She said so in her next note. He said he understood, then, about the stain, too. The next couple of weeks they wrote all about wet dreams. It was great.

He told her he was sorry to hear about what had happened with the boys. But if she was embarrassed, that's all it was—embarrassment. It would go away. The laughing always goes away, but the thing, the real thing, stays. Kind of, she was a woman now. She wrote back and said, kind of, he was a man. They didn't write anything the next day.

Then everything got funnier. Og started calling their whole set up the "com-post office," and the cow, the real Ogie, was their "leather carrier."

Whenever she didn't get a letter she said that Og better be careful or she was going to send her complaints to the "ground beef department."

"Beef very careful," he said, "there's a lot at steak."

"You know, I've probably pasteurize in school."

"And I didn't notice you? You must be pasture prime."

"Calf a heart, will you. I can't take these chops."

"Bull."

And so it went. A very quick week. And just as quickly, it turned.

Mari got the latest letter.

"Let's meat," it said. And there was more: "No really, let's meet. I guess we have to. It's time." He knew, now, who she was. And she didn't. This was his way of telling her. "It's that part about being fair to each other," finished the note.

So here she was, walking out of the house. To the meeting. He chose this Saturday which was, she thought, lucky. She didn't have to explain to anyone. And getting the tortillas was easy enough. She would go there first, then head back by the long way beside the pasture. Where *he* would be. Og. Whoever he was. Whatever would happen.

It was true. She did want to see him. Everything was going so well, so perfect. The whole thing was a happy secret. But all the secrets she had were good and bad. Bad's turn had come, maybe. She felt heavy in her Nikes, really for the first time. No flying today. She couldn't get her permanent, which was getting old now, to come out right. It felt higher on one side of her head. What a day. *But she should be happy,* she kept telling herself. *Real happy.* She looked like one of her ballerina pictures, the one with the lady tired out and sweating and hair all on one side. She wished she looked better. When her cousin came, she said she wished she looked as good as Mari. Ha. Her dog followed her part way, but she sent him back. He looked at her and just sat there. She was starting to feel stuffed. More even than the worst times. *Happy happy happy.*

She walked, saying *hap-py hap-py* with each step. She got to the *tortillería.* Mrs. Sandoval charged the tortillas—two dozens, right? She said it just like her mother. They were still hot. There was moisture in the plastic the tortillas came in, and the smell was…no, she couldn't think about it. Stop trying to guess. Just keep walking. She made the turn so she could see the pasture. The cows. Him.

No. No one was there. But she was looking, she couldn't help but look, her breath was taken away, she was afraid at first, she started laughing, she couldn't believe it, how silly, this was wonderful, she couldn't believe it.

All the cows in the field, this field, all the black Black Angus, there must have been thirty at least, in big, white, spraypainted letters all said "I love you" "I love you." Every one. Mari was laughing. She looked around for him. Him.

She saw a letter on Ogie. She ran for it and got out of there as fast as possible, before reading the letter even. The rancher was going to be mad, oh was he. She ran down the road and stopped finally when everything looked safe. She could still see the cows. They were painted on both sides. "I love you" "I love you."

She read the letter. It was really a note, but with a lot of paper used up around the words.

I chickened out. Monday instead, after school.

Oh no, she thought. Again. I'm going to hit him. That's the first thing I'm going to do.

And it drove her crazy.

Really, how bad could this be? "I love you." I love you, too, she thought. What else. Even if she hadn't slept all weekend. She had looked all around school, at every face. She couldn't guess. But it was Monday now, and today she would know. She hoped. If only she knew already. This was too much. This was better than the letters, almost—like the days before the holidays. Who knows. But she wasn't afraid this time. After school she walked. With her friends. Up to the point where she turned to go home. She headed for the long way. They all said goodbye. She hadn't told them. Anything. She saw the jerk guys laughing a ways behind. Nothing could spoil her day today.

She walked. She made the turn. The cows were there. No one had washed them. "I love you." She laughed. She looked around. No one.

She heard the boys still laughing. She wished they'd hurry up and go away. Sometimes one or two of them came this way, but not usually. Of all days, today one did. He was one of the ones who had "seen" her. Oh great. She avoided him—this was Ruben—and Jorge pretty well since then. She would say hi so he wouldn't say anything. Just hurry.

"Hi."

"Hi," he said. He kept walking, like maybe he was in a hurry. Good. then he stopped, and turned around.

"Mari?"

Not now, she thought. Not now. "What?" She was feeling red. Stupid.

"I'm sorry about that time. You know." He looked down at the ground, like he was embarrassed or something. Not now, thought Mari.

"It's okay." Well, okay sort-of. Just not now. She looked around. No one yet. And there was no letter on the cow.

"I didn't want to laugh. Jorge showed me, he pointed. And he started laughing, so I had to. But I didn't want to. I just had to, you know?"

"Thank you. Okay." Why now. Leave. She didn't want to talk about it. Leave. Stupid, she said with her eyes.

"Just so you know."

"Okay," said her voice, but her eyes went crazy, stupid stupid stupid.

"There's no letter, exactly, today."

"What?" Her eyes said that, too. He knew, thought Mari. He had been spying. Jerk jerk *jerk!*

"I'm the beef jerky."

Mari looked at him. Suddenly her eyes were stronger than the rest of her. "Og?"

"What?"

"Nothing, it's stupid." Stupid. She had never said anything to…was this him? No. Oh no.

"Oh." He was looking at her with his whole face now.

"Do you know about the letters?"

"Yeah. It's me." He tried to smile, tried to *make* his mouth smile. He was turning redder than she already was. But he kept looking, like he couldn't look at her enough, like he wanted to see anything, everything she was about to do.

She thought about all the letters. She had some with her in her notebook. Right there in her arms. They were wonderful. The cows were spray painted still. She looked at them, her eyes made her.

"It's true," he said. He was getting worse. Redder.

"Ruben." She walked in front of him. "Ruben?"

He smiled and nodded his head yes.

She nodded her head the other way no. It was too hard to believe, too much.

They both started laughing. It was okay. They laughed and she hit his arm. Okay but stupid. They began walking, to the shade, then farther, where they were alone, a place near where the water ran to the pasture. No one else ever went there. He had talked about it in one of the letters. He was sorry, but that time Jorge had *made* him laugh. Mari said that he was funnier than Jorge. Yes, but Jorge is big. Big big. What could he do? Ah, she said, that's true. He is bigger. Bigger so he could be more stupid. They both laughed.

It took a while, believing. But they talked about the letters. Everything. What had happened getting them and putting them there. About the spray paint. The spray paint. "I love you."

"I do, Mari." His face was redder than a balloon, even before he said it.

By now it felt too late. Mari loved the letters too much. She looked down at her feet. She was wearing sandals today. Her feet felt light. She felt light. She couldn't tell if that felt good or bad now. "Me, too," she said. "You know, I always thought you were a jerk."

She didn't really. Love him.

But he was going to kiss her, she could tell. Stupid stupid stupid. He didn't look like any movie star.

But she closed her eyes, like in the movies, anyway. That's the way they had all talked about how they would do it if they did.

Then they stopped. Before it happened.

They stood there.

No jokes now.

They looked at each other.

"You've got muscles," Mari said as she looked at his arms. She was lying. He was skinnier than a spaghetti.

"You too."

She could tell by the way his face screwed up that even *he* thought that that was a stupid thing to say. It was true, though.

They just stood there.

They didn't look at each other now, but Mari could see him anyway from the sides of her eyes. It hurt to look like that, but she wanted to be ready for whatever happened. She took a breath, and just in time—she hadn't been breathing, she realized, for a long, long time.

So. There she was, and there was he. He was looking at her now, she could tell from her sideways eyes. She hoped she was pretty, she guessed. She thought she was, and wanted him to think so too, after all this time. She couldn't think of anything else to think.

Except this: she turned around to look straight at his eyes, or really, her eyes pulled her around, as if they were doing the thinking, and they were tired of hurting. If he was going to look, she was too. He looked at her eyes back. Only her eyes, now. They crossed themselves.

But he didn't laugh. He came closer to her, and hugged her. Kind of. That way you hug some people sort of only at the shoulders. For a long time. And she guessed she was hugging him back.

He wanted to kiss her, really. He really wanted to, she thought. And she thought that she wanted him to kiss her, too, she guessed. Things would be all right. Two words, all right. Stupid stupid, dumb. But okay, too.

The letters were worth something, after all.

He chickened out though. Like before, he said. But that wasn't it—this was her eyes doing the thinking again. They knew too much about each other, now. It wasn't chickening out. They just couldn't. Maybe they never would. Ever. With anyone else, even. It was gross. Stupid. They started laughing. Loud and strong and forever. This was so dumb. Both of them said the same thing together, and laughed even more until it hurt, but a lot.

"I do love you, you know," he said, sort of, again. But he wasn't going to kiss her, thought her eyes.

"Me too." She looked at her feet again. She moved them, but it was as if they weren't really connected to her. She really loved the letters. A whole lot. She said so.

"Me too," he said. They really loved each other this way. In the letters.

He would probably never hug her again, she thought. Not more than he just did. And not the same way. Like friends now, or like Mari and her grandmother. Closer, but fake, like it would go away real quick and you knew it. She didn't mean that in a bad way, just the way it really felt.

He hugged her, then. And she was right.

They spoke, kind of about other stuff now.

"I didn't think you were Mexican, so I never said anything in Spanish in the letters."

"Me neither," said Ruben. "And then when I guessed who you were, I still didn't because I thought you might guess about me."

She never would have guessed *him,* she thought. Even if he *had* written something in Spanish. It would have reminded her of her cousin, who could speak perfectly. The letters were perfect like that. Not like Ruben spoke. So, thought Mari, they would never get together as she dreamed. Like movies. Not really. Not after today. Even if they tried.

"I had a good time with them. I watched you sometimes, right from here. Remember? I called it my 'steak out.'" They both laughed.

"Yes." So she knew who wrote the letters finally. She looked at him. She couldn't help it—they were friends now, like it or not. Even if the letters didn't go on. Even if anything. They would probably try stuff for a while, but.... Even if it didn't work, though, they still had something, something they could hold in their hands. That could never go away. Ruben could, but not the letters.

It was time to go, time for dinner, and her mother would be worrying, and Ruben's mother.

"Shake," said Ruben. He did a bunch of stuff with his hands.

"Shake," said Mari. But she stopped his hands with her eyes, stupid, they said, and she held them both with hers, but only real quick. She wouldn't have missed this, not for anything, she thought, even if they took off her braces. She picked up her notebook. She thought about kissing him on the cheek and running away, like in the movies. Naw, that was stupid. The stupidest.

Goodbye. Tomorrow they would see each other, tomorrow, they said, laughing. How embarrassing. They wouldn't be able to tell anyone, not anyone. He better not.

Goodbye, and Mari had to be careful as she walked away—the sandals and the pasture. Where there was no one before, she thought, where there was only a red face—a super red face—now she had a friend. Someone to talk to. In secret. Real stuff. Maybe. Ruben.

But Ruben of all the people!

The jerk.

She was so embarrassed. But he was right, the embarrassment, the red, it would go away. Especially now.

72

No! Being embarrassed was stupid.

No, everything was stupid.

No—well, she couldn't figure it out. Maybe you had to think of all this as braces, that it would all work out. Then again....Stupid stupid stupid, just everything.

But she laughed anyway, as she walked away, and he couldn't hear her, laughed longer than the longest train whistle anywhere, because she felt good, and when she got home she just kept right on laughing, but inside herself now, like the way spaghetti, all the spaghettis, feel going down inside into you. Just like that. Laughing and laughing, inside, loud and strong and forever.

Stupid stupid stupid stupid. She felt great.

Then They'd Watch Comedies

"Leocadio, you've been fighting again."

"Yes, mama."

"What happened? You look terrible."

"They were calling me 'Leo' again."

"No."

"Yes."

"And you fought?"

"Yes."

"Did you win?"

"Yes."

She took a deep breath, too loud to be real breathing. "Get cleaned for dinner. I'll make your favorite."

"I really beat that other guy up."

His mother nodded from side to side, but smiled. "Wait till I tell your father."

"He will be proud, no?"

"Yes."

He *was* proud, and said so, and hit Leocadio on the side of the chin, and even though it hurt, Leocadio smiled. He had done right, now, finally. He had found someone, smaller, who was dumb enough to tease him when he was alone, no guys to back him, so Leocadio beat him up, beat him up good. Finally. Leocadio was as proud as his father, or because of his father, and he was going to look for that guy again tomorrow, maybe. Maybe he would steal his girlfriend, too.

Everyone sat at the table to eat, and Leocadio was smiling.

"Potatoes *con huevo* for that son of mine. You could smell them cooking, no?"

"Yes."

"Of course he could," said his father to his mother, or to himself, "that's a smart head on that son, yes." His father hit him, a little harder, on the chin again, pretending he was a boxer.

"That hurts," said Leocadio this time. His hands stayed on the table and did not try to protect his face.

"Yes, but it feels good, no? Where are the girls tonight?"

"Babysitting. Oh, Leocadio, Julieta wants you to walk her home tonight. She'll call when she is ready. You'll do it?" his mother raised her eyes to ask, as she served the dinner.

"Yes, but I don't see what she's so worried about. She's so ugly nobody will ever try..."

"Leocadio!" his mother interrupted him.

"No, really, even if it was boot black and they were sure not to get caught..."

"Leocadio!" again. His mother put her hands on her hips.

"And somebody paid them to..."

"Le-o-ca-dio!" this time.

"Where did it happen?"

"What, papa?"

"Where did you hit this guy?"

"In the parking lot. A bunch of my guys..."

"No, I mean, on the face? Did you hit him on the face or just push each other around until somebody tripped like a bunch of, you know, *jotitos?*"

"No, I hit him, papa. He was bleeding all over the place. On his shirt."

"Leocadio," said his mother. She was not yelling. Or laughing, now.

"And then I hit him again before I left because he wouldn't promise not to call me Leo."

"So you hit him again?"

"Yes, papa."

"Did you hear that," said his father, looking at his mother this time, "another Reies Madero. That's what we have here, another Madero, but one that doesn't lose."

"It was only one fight, papa. I only ever got beat up before. Every time."

"Eat your dinner, Leocadio, it will get cold. You too," said his mother to his father. She put some tortillas that she had been warming on the table, and took one out for each of them.

"Where are the girls tonight?" asked his father. Leocadio looked at his mother.

"Babysitting. And Leocadio, I want you to leave Maricela alone when she's with her boyfriend this time."

"But mama, they're all by themselves in there when she is babysitting. Do you want something to happen? More babies, maybe?"

"Leocadio!" said his mother.

"Just because she finally gets a boyfriend you're so worried for her. She's only eighteen, what does she know?"

"But Leocadio, you're only fourteen," said his mother.

"I know, and 'what do I know.'"

"What do you know?" said his father. "Ha. Reies Madero sits here and says 'what do I know.' Chh, what a joke." His father laughed, by himself, and hit him on the chin. Never a real laugh, hardly ever, he couldn't even remember when, thought Leocadio.

"Eat," said his mother.

"But my jaw hurts," said Leocadio.

"Ha, hurts. What did you do to that other guy, anyway? What did you say his name was?"

"It was..."

"Besides making him bleed. I mean, why was he bleeding? Teeth? Nose? Both? Ha, lower?"

"Ay, no. Leocadio, you didn't?"

"Like they all did to me, mama, all those times. I just hit him, papa. I don't know what I did. I don't know where."

"And he bled, no?"

"Yes."

"What was his name," asked his mother, this time.

"I don't know. I think he's still in Junior High."

"White?" asked his father.

"Yes."

"But not after you left him. Chh."

"Is he okay?" Maybe this was worse than she thought.

"I don't know, but I hope not."

"Leocadio!"

"Madero!" said his father, and tried to hit him again. It was too hard, and Leocadio moved his chin to miss most of it.

"I don't care, mama. They were all calling me Leo, and they wouldn't stop. I kept yelling but they wouldn't."

"So you beat them up, yes?" asked his father.

76

"No, I just kept yelling first. Then they left except for that one guy who came out and yelled 'Leo Leo Leo Leo, for his breakfast he drinks pee-o!' and I told him to cut it out because..."

"You were alone, no?" asked his father. He was smiling. But it was a father smile, the kind he gave to other men when his wife wasn't looking. Leocadio's stomach got tighter.

"No, there were some other guys, some friends of mine, Johnny and the others. But I told this guy I didn't care what he said like that..."

"What!" No smile now.

"I mean like 'pee-o' and that stuff. Just that he better not call me Leo, just like you said, papa, because that's not my name, not like that, right? I told him he'd better call me Leocadio or else. I told him, a lot of times."

"Leocadio," said his mother. Just like that.

"So you hit him?" asked his father.

"No, not until I asked him what he was going to call me and he said 'Leo' again. Then I hit him. I beat him up."

"Hooo, you showed him. Chh. That will teach him."

"No!" Leocadio shook his head hard, aimed at his father, then got up and left the table.

"Leocadio!" his mother said.

"Where are the girls, anyway?" asked his father, finishing dinner.

Afterward, Leocadio's father washed the dishes, and Leocadio came out of his room to dry. His father would do the dishes, but took no care to clean the grease, the colors from the chips in the plates or the rims of the glasses. Leocadio rubbed them off, the color of potato, of ketchup. The rubbing made a sound like a cat that thinks it's about to get stepped on, but realizes after its first noise, no, still safe.

"The girls should be doing this. Chh," said Leocadio's father, shaking his head from side to side and showing Leocadio the front of his shirt, which was wet.

"They're working." The argument was old, and everyone had been through it. The women should be doing this, the women should be doing that, said his father. But he only worked part-time. They brought in the money, the real money. Leocadio's mother worked at S.H. Kress, and had worked there since high school. The girls were always babysitting, and had been babysitting since before they were women, before almost they could tie their own shoes.

"Still, this is a woman's job, Leocadio. Where is your mother?"

"Washing."

"She should be watching this. Two grown men washing dishes. Washing dishes! Chh."

"I'm only fourteen."

"After today? Ha. Only a man does what you did, beating up those guys like that."

Leocadio shook his head. "One guy. He was smaller than I was, you know. And I think maybe they made him say those things. The other guys he was with before, I mean."

"Made them bleed."

"Because he wouldn't say my name, papa. Like what happened to you when they called *you* 'Leo'—or tried to call you Leo—when you were a kid and came here. Tell me again how you took care of them, all those kids that called you that."

"Beat them up."

Leocadio's mother came into the room with an arm full of clothes. She shook her head as she listened to the last part of the conversation. The clothes she held were mostly women's clothes. "You have nothing more you need washed?"

"Always washing," said Leocadio's father. "You should stop that and wash the dishes, or not use so many dishes. Always grease. You get them so dirty."

"I have to look clean. And you, too. Where are your clothes?"

"There aren't any."

"What do you mean?"

"I didn't dirty any."

They all went quiet. Clean clothes meant no work, and to talk about no work was to talk about the weather—warm, hot, snowing, it didn't matter. It couldn't be changed now. Leocadio motioned to his mother that she was holding his only dirty clothes, so she left the room. She had no time to go through it all now. She had spent half of her life talking about the weather.

"Should be washing dishes," said his father under his breath to Leocadio as his mother left. Leocadio kept drying. "Knocked the shit out of them is what I did," continued his father.

Later, Leocadio's father came out of his room in his underpants to watch TV. He did that whenever the girls weren't home. Everyone watched TV at night, but they always had to watch what Leocadio's father chose. Always a police story. Sometimes a western. Leocadio liked comedies better, and so did his mother, and so did his sisters. The nights his father left and came back drunk or with other men were almost worth the shouting. Sometimes his mother gave his father money. He always got so angry after this that he'd go out again and get more drunk because he said that *he* should be giving *her* money. She couldn't win. She'd say, then, what for? she didn't drink, and he would get even angrier and say that all she was good for was three children, no more, that was no wife, and then he would go out with horse legs, the way a big horse brings all the weight of his body down on each hoof. It was all right, his mother would say. Then they'd watch comedies, Leocadio and his mother and his sisters. It hurt, but sometimes it was better.

Now his father turned the channels. Leocadio watched the bluegreen Virgin of Guadalupe, massive on his forearm, Channel 9, 10, her head turned, 11, her eyes. "There, this one." And hair coming through her, all over, a blanket, high grass. She was always warm. His father went back to the couch which, when he was home, was all his.

"You have a hole in your *calzones,*" said Leocadio's mother to his father. She had been watching, too.

His father looked down at his underwear. "So, I told you last week and you still haven't fixed them, and what's happened to the girls, anyway? Are they too good for this kind of work? Hole in everybody's head! Except for Leocadio there." He was talking to no one, no one was in the room except Leocadio, and he wasn't talking *to* him. "He *puts* holes in people's heads, other people's heads, where they belong." He reached for an unopened Coors on the shelf next to the couch. He had finished one, but always brought two cans so that he would not have to get up. No one would bring beer for him anymore, no matter how much he shouted. The night was beginning, like others.

"Not other 'people's' heads, papa. One guy. And I doubt it was a hole. And he was smaller than I was, a lot smaller. And they made him do it. And he never *would* call me Leocadio. And you'll probably get a note from school, or a call or something because they'll say I was picking on him."

"Well, maybe it was a hole. You can't say about these things."

"No."

"Humph. But it bled. I mean, you hurt him."

"Yes. A lot."

"Leocadio, stop now." His mother had been in and out of the room, sometimes putting away clothes, sometimes watching TV. She looked tired tonight, thought Leocadio. More than usual.

"But I didn't enjoy it papa, not really. I mean, I really did hurt him. It hurt enough to hit him. I'm sore."

Leocadio's father looked at him and nodded his head up and down, without words. Yes, up, down. Yes, slowly.

79

"It wasn't worth it, papa."

Leocadio's father looked at him and said, "It was," but turned back to the TV even before he had finished.

Leocadio shook his head from side to side, without words, trying to speak the other language, too.

His mother, father, and Leocadio watched TV for a long time. It was almost time for the news. His father's head was back, chin up so that it almost touched his eyelashes.

"Hey," said his mother to his father, "don't go to sleep. Maricela will be home soon. And it's almost time for you," she looked at Leocadio, "to go get Julieta."

"Okay," said Leocadio.

"Hey," said his mother to his father again, "get dressed or go to bed." His father made a noise from somewhere between languages. Sometimes he got stuck there. "Did you get a check this week?" She had forgotten to ask.

"Yes, I got one. One dollar, that's what I got, one."

"Silly," said his mother. "Where is it? I'm going to the bank tomorrow."

"In my pants. Go get it, will you," his father motioned to Leocadio with his head, the way men do.

Leocadio went into his parents' bedroom to get the check, and came back with it in his hands.

"Papa," said Leocadio.

His father spoke a noise from the space between languages again. He spoke from the lost place a father and a son never share together, but both use. Especially those with the same name.

"Give it to me, Leocadio," said his mother.

"Wait. Papa."

"What do you want," asked his father, but only as a half-question.

"This check says 'Leo' on it."

"Come here, Leocadio, just give it to me," said his mother.

"Mama, stop it. Papa?"

"What?" said his father, trying to close his eyes like before. It didn't look the same.

"This check says 'Leo' on it."

"It's a check. Give it to your mother."

Leocadio dropped the check and looked. "PAPA!" he yelled.

"Leocadio!" His mother tried to turn him from his direction, from his words.

80

"Papa, it says, 'LEO' on it!"

His father raised himself on an elbow, like the women in old movies. "'LEO!'"

"Leocadio," said his mother, without volume. His father waved at her to stop.

"It does, it says that," said his father.

"But you've worked there enough times, a lot of times. They know, they *have* to know."

"I'm not sure." He shrugged his shoulders. His whole body moved, too much for the motion of shrugging.

"Papa!"

"Leocadio, stop!" His father raised his voice. "You stop yelling, what have I taught you, if you *ever* yell at your mother..."

"What have you taught me? What have you *taught* me? And I *wasn't* yelling at my mother. That has nothing to do..."

"Stop it, Leocadio. It says 'Leo' on it. What do you think I am, stupid?" He sat up. "You think I am so stupid that I can't see that the women work in this house and that the men stay at home?"

"What stupid?"

"Yes, stupid. It says 'Leo' on it, it does, I know it. It could say 'asshole' on it and I'd still take it."

"Ay, no," said his mother. Leocadio wished she wasn't here.

He shook his head, "But..."

"No, you've been doing all the yelling. It's my turn. Twelve-year-old, fourteen, whatever. I've worked all my life, Leocadio, starting when I was younger than you are, with pain." Leocadio clicked his teeth and dropped into a chair. "So, so you've heard that, so what. When I was young a man, a black man, I worked with black men, a kind of work that wasn't nice, that's the kind of work I had to do, he told me, 'If you got your head in the lion's mouth you better use your other hand to pet it.' That's what he said and I never forgot it. You know what that means?"

Leocadio turned his face.

"Oh, that's pretty, turn away, sure. *I* can't. *I* got a family. You know what that means? It means that I could leave that family all alone, start again, but I never would. It means I could give up everything, but I never would. It means there's a way out, real easy, staring everybody in the face but that doesn't make it like, whatever, the right way. Chh."

"Letting them call you Leo sounds pretty easy. Real easy. Get off it."

"No. No, that's the hardest. You don't know what the hard way is, you've just got to realize..."

"*I've* got to realize? I almost got killed out there today, and I almost killed. He was bleeding."

"I'm sorry. But you didn't kill him. You don't know what that is…"

"Bleeding because he wouldn't do what you told me he *should* do, *had* to do."

"I'm sorry, well…"

"No you're not, you loved it."

"No, I…"

"You loved it. That's all you could talk about."

"It hurt."

"Hurt? Hurt? You're a liar!"

"Leocadio!" his mother could only say.

"No, no, you're right. It felt good. Felt good to make you a man. You could be a man."

"For who? For who, papa? It hurt me, it still hurts, my jaw hurts, from where he hit me, from where *you* hit me even."

"Me. It's true. It felt good. It felt good for me."

"Oh thanks, papa, thank you a lot." Leocadio turned his head fast, as a batter turns to get a call after not swinging.

"Thanks papa is right, that's right. You *should* thank me. You should thank me for *not* fighting, for *not* getting bloody, for *not* getting my jaw hurt."

"Thank you for *what?* I can't believe what you're saying."

"We're alive, we're here. You can *fight!*"

"Is that what you've given me, is this a gift? Is that what it is? A Christmas present?"

"But *you can fight!*"

"Fight? Who wants to? And for what? What now? That kid still didn't call me Leocadio, papa. I fought to get the same results you do, only I hurt more. I hurt a lot more. For nothing."

"Hurt? Ha. It feels good, you just don't know." His father showed his teeth, but not really like a smile. It didn't work. Leocadio wanted to shout at it.

"Papa, it doesn't. It doesn't feel good."

"It does." And he was in his underwear.

Leocadio shook his head. His neck felt strong, but because it was tight. "You don't fight, you get along, but that doesn't make it right. *I* fight, I don't get along, but is *that* right? No," his neck felt strong, still, the wrong way, "no, it isn't uh uh. I don't want it."

"It will make you different than I am. More."

"Anything is more. I can take the middle and I am more, too. And it doesn't hurt. I don't bleed. No fighting, no getting along, nothing. Just moving. Just not talking."

"There is no middle." His father shook his head, slowly this time. The other language.

"There is." Leocadio could not hear those other words, but he, too, could speak them. With his whole body, by the roots of his neck, he nodded his head up and down, now, yes and yes.

"No one lives on a bridge, Leocadio."

"Unless he has to, papa, unless that's the only place left, unless that's the only place that doesn't hurt."

"Then I named you right, Leocadio. Twelve, fourteen, you will see. You're no different from me."

"I'm going to get Julieta."

La Boda

Tonio farted a fart wide, one that shoved its way through that room like something it might have taken the Colorado River thousands of years to do, Grand Canyon-size, a champ.

"Where's the TV thing, the TV Guide?" demanded Arturo.

"Ay, *viejo*. It's right on the floor where you left it," answered Lilia. They had both heard Tonio, Tonio the littlest, the most sensitive, the biggest problem to reward them after such good lives they both had led.

"Where is he?"

"In the kitchen."

"Ay, *m'ija*, not with the food again."

"I can't keep him in his room, *viejo*." They had been all through that, and the embarrassment too of the visit to the doctor and what happened in the waiting room. No, it was too much. And no answers.

"He's going to fart at the wedding, you know he's going to do it big at the wedding, Lilia."

"Stop cussing in front of me. You keep saying that, stop it." She never would get used to the word. She didn't even have a word of her own for it. It simply happened and didn't deserve a name, this noise-making. It was terrible, and their own son, ay no, not like this. "The doctor said it would stop, anyway." She said it too quietly.

"In time, *m'ija*, in time. But not in time for *la boda*, the wedding. Not nearly in time."

Lilia clicked her tongue. Tonio let loose again. Big.

"Let it be Ray, please, I already told him."

"But what about Jaime, Delia? What will Mario say?"

84

"Jaime's married, mama. So what do we do about his wife? Are we supposed to leave her out? Now they can both be in it." Delia looked at the list in front of her. It would all work out perfectly, now. If Jaime agreed—Mario would convince him and she would convince Mario—and if Jaime's parents Arturo and Lilia would say yes, too, that they would also be in the wedding then it would be perfect. The invitations could be printed, finally. Arturo and Lilia would say yes, of course they would say yes. And El Casino was already scheduled for the reception.

"Okay, okay, *Madre Santa!* But are you sure you want little Jorge to be the ring bearer?"

"Yes, he is going to look so cute."

"Ha, he's not your brother, what do you know? Wait and see, if you *can* see him. Maybe he will leave his mud at home? Do you think?"

"Ma-ma!"

"De-li-a," she mimicked.

It was a good lunch. It must have been, because he exploded. Loud.

"*¿Otro pedo?*" yelled his father from the living room. "At least get out of the kitchen, Tonio, *por favor!*" He was not asking nicely but it didn't matter to Tonio. Not any more, not when he finally realized. This farting was a power, "*pedo* power" his brother Jaime called it, and it was a very worthwhile thing to do. It meant that he had eaten good food, that he didn't have to go to first grade, that he had a room of his own which no one else in the whole town, probably, could brag about. It meant I am special, thought Tonio, and he was proud, sort of. Red-faced but proud. And he had gotten used to the smell.

Of course, only his little cousin Jorge from next door would play with him, and he *had* to play with Tonio because no one would play with *him*, either. He was always dirty. Dirty so that there was always mud on him somewhere any time of the day no matter how many baths they gave him. He was too young to go to school still and so he and Tonio fell naturally together. Tonio was the leader, though. Farting is much more impressive. Jorge didn't care about the smell. He always said he didn't smell anything. In fact, it made him laugh, and Tonio appreciated this. It was not the mean laugh other people laughed sometimes, it was a real laugh. Occasionally there was not enough space in a room for the noise from Tonio's power and Jorge's laughing to fit. Tonio from his bottom, then Jorge from his mouth, then Tonio from his mouth, and so on. Dominoes. And sometimes Tonio was asked to take a bath with Jorge because it was the only way Jorge would take one without a life or death

85

struggle. Tonio would always agree, because it was the opinion of Jorge that Tonio's farting under water was incomparable. That was, in fact, the opinion of everyone.

"I'm sorry, Jaime, I chickened out." Mario shrugged his shoulders. "I promised Delia her cousin Ray could be best man, and I promised her mother even more so. But listen, now you and Anna can be *padrinos*. Take your pick, *padrinos* of anything you want, it doesn't matter. That's the deal."

"It's okay, don't worry. It's better this way, especially for you, later, you know? I mean *much* later, in the night. Take my word for it." They both laughed. "Ray's the guy in the Navy, right?"

"Yeah. He's coming in special. Delia's real excited."

"Did you ever meet him?"

"Yes, once. But I know him perfectly the way Delia talks about him. Too perfectly."

"Maybe he'll come with us to Paco's for your party. Does he drink?"

"He's in the Navy, asshole."

"So, another wedding, Delia and Mario now, and they want us to be *padrinos*."

"Of course they do, *vieja*. We give presents."

"Arturo!"

"So, it's wedding season again. *La boda* lives. Same as baseball season, have you ever noticed? No matter what they try to do to it. And everyone wants to be in the World Series of weddings. That's why they want us to be *padrinos,* even if it's just *padrinos* in charge of toilet paper for the wedding. It will be pink, listen to me, and soft. Chh. Ever since that *boda* where we gave the big silver punch bowl. Boy, if only they knew we had gotten it free and had to give it because we couldn't afford to buy anything else. And if only we could tell everyone, then we wouldn't have to keep worrying about how we have to keep giving just a little more each time. And this time your sister's daughter. Money. Maybe we could afford Europe, if they wouldn't be too insulted?" Arturo shook his head. Too many times.

"Stop it, it's a wedding."

"It's money. Silly." More shaking.

"Arturo…"

86

"And did you forget about Tonio? You know what he's going to do, you know it."

Lilia took a breath, the long-short kind, an *eeegh!* "Ay, don't say it, I know, I know. But it's okay, Jorge will be there, we won't be the only ones with problems. They have to take him, and not only because it's his brother getting married but because Delia, that Delia, wants him and only him to be the ring bearer. What a day it's going to be!" She clicked her tongue.

"Maybe we can think of some way..."

"I already accepted, Arturo. I had to, after all."

"Had to, humph. What, had to." He pressed his lips together.

"And Raymundo will be there. He's going to be best man."

"What about Jaime? I though he and Mario were..."

"Well, Delia wanted to include Anna, so they are going to be *padrinos,* too."

"The World Series."

"So your brother is getting married, Jorge."

"Yes." Jorge was not at all cheerful.

"And I heard you are going to carry the rings."

"Yes."

"So what's wrong? Are you nervous? Come on."

"No."

Tonio looked at him, then started to run toward the arroyo. "Come on," he yelled, "then, let's go."

Jorge followed after him, but tripped.

"Aw Jorge, stop yelling, it doesn't hurt that much. I know. And they'll hear you. You don't want that, do you?" They weren't supposed to go into the arroyo. The flash floods in Tucson come like brown walls in summer. Full of stuff, boards and stumps and wagons. Or like the Tasmanian Devil in Bugs Bunny, moving and growling like that.

"No, but it does hurt, I don't care what you say."

They headed straight for Their Place. It was where two mesquite trees hung over the arroyo from opposite banks so that, after the two boys had cleared off all the little branches and webs, there was a natural bridge across the water, when there *was* water. Sometimes sewage ran through and so their parents didn't want them down there then either. But for now the two boys knew better. There would be only rain water from up in the mountains and it wasn't the season, yet, for flash floods. They knew about these things. Plenty of reason, then, for a club, their club, for the "Aztecs of America." And besides, they had a secret.

It was a gun. With two bullets. So what if it was rusty. And old. And hadn't worked even though they had tried. They would get it to work, sometime. But they had to wait for a special reason, a special occasion, and that's why they had it on the little shelf. A specially carved little shelf, perfect, with two smaller shelves, one for each of the bullets. With a blanket that sparkled, which Jorge had kept from under the last Christmas tree. All this in a small side-cave carved into the bank of the arroyo, specially, with a door made of the mesquite branches from the two big trees bundled and tied together. The cave was almost right on the spot where they had found the gun. And both of them wanted to use the gun, a lot, so they decided that neither would use it after the first couple of attempts. It was too special, too neat, a secret. It had to be taken care of good. They were sure it was a secret. That's what secrets were, stuff they couldn't take home. Stuff that would always get taken away.

"What do you mean, why marry?"

"Hey, it's okay, you know? Everyone's growing up," said Ray, the Ray.

"Not that much," said Mario. "Her parents would kick her out, and my parents would never let me bring her home."

"How will you feel, Delia, leaving flowers for the Virgin? How will you be honoring *that?*" Ray's eyebrows jumped up and down.

"Don't be silly," answered Delia, "I'll be leaving flowers because I'm sorry for her." All three laughed.

"Hey, you're tough, *prima,* but not that tough. I'm in the Navy, after all. Tougher." Ray opened his mouth and pointed: "Look, an anchor tattooed to the back of my throat. *That's tough.*" More laughter.

"I didn't know you could get tattoos like that in San Diego," said Mario.

Ray moved his lips and moved his head left and right, mimicking Mario. "You can get anything you want, brother."

"Ay, Ray, the Navy hasn't changed you!" Delia hit his arm, but not with a fist exactly.

"Are you kidding? I joined the Navy so the world could see *me!*"

"Booo. That's really old, Ray, come on."

"Old as the hills on grandma's chest!"

"First time I heard that I laughed so hard I fell off my dinosaur," Mario smiled.

"Cute, but ugly. I'm the one in the Navy so I can get away with this, you can't. You gotta be tough to say these things." Everyone laughed.

"Ay, Ray," sighed Delia.

"No, *I* Ray, *you* Delia."

Mario grimaced. "Me sick."

"What, pregnant already?"

Lilia read the invitation, looking for their names first. "Here it is, Arturo. Look how big this will be, everyone will be there, I think."

"Everyone. It looks like a scorecard. What a time to be out robbing." He looked at the outside of the invitation, a picture of a bride and groom with her veil covering their faces as they kissed in the woods. "A new creation, two of us/ Like the dawning of the perfect day. Shee-it."

"ARTURO!"

"And that's what they do in the woods. I knew it." He opened the invitation and skimmed: Mr. and Mrs., and Mr. Mrs., invite the honour—who spells like that, honour?—of your presence... "Presents, Lilia, presents, I told you!" at the marriage of their daughter, son, and cordially invite you and your family to a religious ceremony on, at St. John's Catholic Church at, Best Man: Raymundo, *Padrinos de Lazo:* Jaime and Anna, *Padrinos de Ramo:* Arturo and Lilia, Ring Bearer: Jorge...Reception at El Casino Ballroom...9:00 P.M., Please Present Invitation. Or Present, thought Arturo. "I guess I'll have to rent a tuxedo, too." Wear a tie. This was work.

"Arturo, of course, and I'll have to make a dress."

"There's no money, Lilia."

"Oh, shush. There is if we don't go to any more weddings, or at least, if we don't give any more presents or be *padrinos.* Not this year."

"Oh sure. Have the World Series first, then work backwards, and since we already know who won we won't have to go to any other games. Perfect."

"*Cállate,* Arturo! Oh, and you know what? Delia says there will be no rehearsal."

"No rehearsal?" Lilia shook her head no. "Of course not, they already know how," Arturo winked.

"*Ay, ¡qué horrible!* Don't even say such a thing. She's wearing white. I asked."

"And the presents won't hurt," said her mother. Delia shook her head.

"Ay, mama. You're making this all so big, even though you *know*. It's all so big, I don't recognize it."

Her mother lowered her head as if to keep on reading. "Everyone should have a wedding."

"Every parent, you mean."

"Ay, Delia."

"Oh mama, I don't mean it, I guess. I kind of think I'm having fun. I just don't want to make it more than it is."

"And what about your father, anyway? Would you care to explain not having a wedding to him?" This wasn't really a question.

"Stop it, we've already been through all this. I wouldn't hurt my daddy for anything."

"Ay, *hija*."

"Oh, it's all okay."

"Okay? You having that Raymundo for best man. Humph!"

"Well, I should have something to say, after all. You know, *you* practically accepted this proposal for me. I wasn't even sure I wanted to get married."

"Delia!"

"Oh, mama, I'm not a child. You were so glad that Mario proposed. 'Un hombre no compra la vaca cuando está agarrando la leche gratis,' that's what you said to me, a man won't buy the cow when he's getting the milk free. I'm not a cow. But what relief there was on your face! I couldn't believe it. It was *almost* worth a wedding just to see that look."

"¡Eres imposible!" Her mother shook her head, *ay no*.

"Well, everyone's okay, you've seen the family. Jorge still breathes mud. Oh, and did you know about little Tonio, my cousin next door?"

"No, what about him?" asked Ray.

"Well," Delia smiled. She wouldn't say.

Ray asked with his hands.

All right then. "He farts."

"He farts? He, oh, he *farts*! That is fantastic! Oh, this is great! A built-in whoopee cushion."

"Ray…"

"When did this start? Like what do you mean, a lot?"

"I don't know, a while back, and there doesn't seem to be anything they can do. And yes. A lot."

"Oh, thank you God, thank you, you *do* exist! Oh wait till church, ohboyohboyohboyoh!"

"That's terrible, Ray. Really."

"Oh, Delia, don't be silly. This could be the best wedding I've ever been to! Oh, no one's going to believe it. It's going to be too good."

"But it's *my* wedding, thank you so much. And poor Toñito, Ray. After all. He's just a little guy and everyone laughs at him. They have had to keep him out of school."

"Boy, does he know how to operate. I should take him back into the Navy with me. What a technique."

"Ray…"

"Oh, Delia, I'll be good. Don't worry, *prima.*" Ray laughed some more. "No really, I will."

"And my brother Jaime and Anna are going to be *padrinos* of something. Ha, Jaime only ever makes fun of me." Tonio shrugged his shoulders.

"Yes," answered Jorge. Neither knew what a *padrino* was.

"Jorge, what is wrong with you?" They were sitting in the cave, which was barely big enough to hold them. They would sit there until Tonio farted, then they had to move out into the air because it was too strong, even for them. There are limits.

"Well, Mario's getting married, and…."

Jorge paused for a good while. "And what," asked Tonio. Something was wrong, he could tell.

Jorge didn't answer right away. "I have no present, nothing to give him."

"Dummy, kids don't have to give presents." Tonio shook his head. He laughed, and it sounded louder in the cave. Too loud, maybe, so that the echo almost hurt.

"I know that, Tonio, I know. But I want to."

"Oh." He guessed it really wasn't funny.

"My parents are giving him, and Delia too, a bunch of stuff. All wrapped up, and they wouldn't let me touch."

"My parents are giving them some forks and spoons and that kind of stuff. And some money, I think. They're something in the wedding so I guess they have to." Jorge was something in the wedding, too. And Tonio was, almost, because everyone else in his family was. But they let him out of it. Whew!

"Yeah, they're something, I don't know what. But see, everyone is giving something."

"I'm not," said Tonio, but thought that maybe he should, now, too.

He hadn't thought about it before. Maybe this was some magic, something grown-up, something people didn't laugh at. "Cheer up, Jorge, we'll think of something." A gift. Nobody can laugh at you if you do that.

"Well, I already thought of something," Jorge said, avoiding Tonio's eyes. He changed positions in the cramped space.

"Oh? What?"

Jorge looked up at the gun.

Tonio didn't answer at first. "But we can't do that, I mean, I mean, come on, it's ours, yours and mine, come on...." Tonio let go, hard.

"Ray, this is Jaime, Delia's cousin."

"Hey, brother," said Ray. Jaime gave him a Raza handshake. "All right."

"He set up the party at Paco's."

"Hey, Jaime, good deal. Can I give you some bucks?" Ray started to take out some money from somewhere in the pant leg of his uniform.

"No, no," Jaime waved him to stop. "You brought enough beer with you there." He pointed to the barrel in the back of Mario's pick-up. "There's going to be plenty of stuff. Are you sure you people from the Navy can handle it?"

"Are you kidding? Of Coors!" They laughed. "But give me beer any day. It doesn't have to be Coors. Is Bud wiser?"

"Booo! But I agree. *La cerveza!*"

"Better than a fart in heaven," Ray laughed. "Oh, sorry," he said, looking at Jaime.

"We told him about Tonio," said Mario.

"Don't be silly," he waved them off to say it was nothing. Not his problem.

"*¡Vámonos!*" yelled Ray, running to the pick-up and pulling a can of beer from behind the barrel. "To the bachelor," he said, raising the can of beer then pouring it all over Mario.

"Shee-it."

"No, Shee-litz!"

Jorge ran back with the tape. Tonio was waiting for him. They added the finishing touches.

It was beautiful. Wrapped up in the sparkly Christmas paper that was almost like cotton and was only a little smudged, either from protecting the gun on the dirt shelf or because of Jorge. His fingers always smudged things.

"Maybe he won't want it and he'll give it back."

"Oh, stop it Jorge. Who wouldn't want it? Wouldn't you like to get it as a present?"

"Yeah. But now we have something, both of us. A wedding present. What about these?"

"Oh, bring them here." They wrapped each of the bullets.

Tonio had done it right away in the car so he and his parents were a little late getting to the church where everyone was set to start. "I'm sorry, we had to get out and open all the windows and wait," said Arturo to Lilia's sister. She smiled and looked down, embarrassed like Lilia. Or for her. Or really, with her. They understood. They knew together what it was like, what no one else could imagine.

Delia came over. "You're a picture, *qué hermosa*," said Lilia. Her sister came over and took her by the arm. "Lilia..." "Ay, your daughter is so pretty." "It's true, Lilia, and I'm so happy. Lilia, I talked to the priest. He said that Tonio could go up into the chorus balcony with the singer, Mrs. García, so that if he did anything the music would probably drown it out. Mrs. García said it was okay." She lifted her eyebrows to see if Lilia would agree. "Of course." "Thank you." "Ah, yes. Yes, of course."

Ray and Mario were off to the side of the church and Arturo walked over and told them everything was ready. Ray gave him an "okay" sign with his fingers. They walked into the church, which was fairly crowded, considering the average number of people who actually go to the church part of a wedding. This was a good sign in predicting how many people would come to the reception. One takes the number of people in church and multiplies by 11.

"Stop it, mama, you're so nervous. Look at daddy, he's okay," said Delia.

"What does he know? Tonio is taken care of. Everything is ready, now. Are you?"

93

The music started. Ray would get his chance to meet the maid of honor, now. With no rehearsal it seemed as if no one knew anyone else. Delia decided it was better this way, not so mushy. And no fighting.

Arturo and Lilia walked in first. They were the *padrinos de ramo,* and so they carried the extra flowers that Delia would leave for the Virgin. Jaime and Anna were the *padrinos de lazo,* and they came next carrying in the *lazo,* the big double-rosary. Then the maid of honor. Then the miniature flower girl tossing white rose petals onto the carpet and Jorge carrying the rings and walking with one muddy shoe, looking from side to side and smiling. He had, after all, a secret. Then Delia, the music, with her mother on her left and her father on her right. It had to be that way, said Delia, the new way. She wanted her mother to walk down the aisle with her, too. The music was in her, and made her walk.

When Delia reached the altar, Mario took her hand and they kneeled together in front of the priest. Ray turned and smiled at the people in church. On the soles of Mario's shoes, in black shoe polish, were painted in perfect order the words "Good" and "bye!" Ray knew it before it happened.

The priest began to speak, but had to stop for a moment as Delia and Mario kneeled because one laugh by one person held inside is inaudible, but many.... The shoes came up. There proceeded a moan, and it wandered around through the pews. But the priest began again, and would not allow it. Delia and Mario and the priest just looked at each other. The priest began again loudly, and everything was all right.

From up in the balcony Mrs. García sang, first quietly then loudly depending on the priest's speeches and everybody whispered how good she was, how perfect. How wonderful for Delia. The first "Ave María" almost got applause. Arturo whispered to Lilia that at least Jaime didn't have to pay for Mrs. García and the priest like he might have had to. It was not so bad that he wasn't the best man. It was cheaper.

Jaime and Anna got up with the *lazo* and went over to the kneeling couple, putting it over their heads and around their shoulders, then stepped back. Delia and Mario stood, and took each other as man and wife, Delia frowning almost horribly as the priest said "wife." Maybe a rehearsal wouldn't have been so bad. She would have words to say about this, most certainly. So many details. Ray winked. Jaime and Anna then took the *lazo* off and went back to sit. Then communion: first Delia and Mario walking up before the altar, then the priest giving communion to the rest of the wedding party, then everyone else. Delia almost did not open her mouth. "Wife" was stuck there. And Mrs. García sang. Jorge wiggled in his seat—this was all too long. "Go in peace," said the priest and it was almost over. Arturo and Lilia brought over the flowers for the Virgin, the *ramo,* and gave them to Delia. She thought for a moment she would not go. Mrs. García started the full length "Ave María." The music pushed Delia over to the left side of the altar where she was to contemplate her final pure moments with the Virgin Mary, leaving flowers as a farewell offering. She had words, inside her head, and stayed too long. Mrs. García took a breath.

pppphhhtt. pht.

It was a fatal breath. Everyone bit his tongue. Delia smiled at the Virgin. Ray started to laugh but Mario kicked him after his first burst. Arturo looked at Lilia and started to say something but she nodded her head no. Delia's mother fanned herself as her father patted his wife on the back it's okay. Why me she breathed, it was too perfect. Jorge stood up on the pew and looked back at the balcony for his friend—he knew it was his friend. *La boda* was ended, and it was time to go. Fast.

The bride and groom stood by the exit, shook hands—or really, watched their hands shake others almost by themselves, as if they were not attached—received the *abrazo,* the hug, from everyone, and reminded all to come to the reception and they said they would, of course, don't be silly, how does it feel. They giggled. A lot of pictures. The fancy ones had already been taken during the wedding by a professional photographer who would be taking more at the reception and who asked if they wanted a picture of that boy in the balcony or not.

It was all too much, thought Tonio. He had heard Ray laugh and he had a plain view of everyone else in St. John's. Even the priest. And now, here at the reception, all the same faces, and more who surely knew by now. Jorge sat with him instead of at the wedding party table, near the presents. They had, at least, a secret.

It was all too funny, said Ray to Mario. Can you believe the timing? Where was Candid Camera when you needed them. A fart. No, the King of Farts right there in church, right at the quietest second. Perfect. But no, said Ray, don't worry. I understand, the poor kid. Hey, he asked, pass the *cerveza.* Mario agreed, poor kid. But it *was* the King, King of all the noises ever.

It was all too, too, I don't know, it's like cussing, I don't know, it's embarrassing, said Lilia to Arturo in a whisper. Arturo answered with a shrug and said that he couldn't believe that his tuxedo went out for $55 a shot. They *should* be shot. It was ridiculous. Did you hear, he wondered, what they would be serving for food? $55, chh. Anyway, I told you he would.

They had all marched in time to the wedding music played by Los Lovers, Mr. Chavez's band, as they entered this place, El Casino. This was the home of all weddings, it had swallowed hundreds and everyone was comfortable here among the permanent decorations. It was all okay, now, thought Delia. Nothing so terrible, except how poor Toñito must feel. At least there was plenty of music, noise, here. Good.

Why me, asked Delia's mother. All night long.

Otra cerveza, yelled Ray.

After the first waltz, everyone danced: *cumbias,* "El Jarabe Tapatillo," "modern." Two teenagers did a new dance, touching places, and everyone stared. They were only kids, can you imagine? Don't be silly, mama! Who would invent a thing like that? ¡*Otra cerveza!* And dressed like a pachuco, that's a zoot suit, look at the chain. Mama! Then came the mariachis.

Mariachi Santa Cruz came to give the *serenata* to the bride as Los Lovers watched. Then the Dollar Dance, and everyone lined up except Ray, who almost had to be held up. That stupid guy, said Tonio. Yeah, said Jorge. They were more interested in the silver-flecked package on the presents' table.

He used a ten dollar bill, Lilia, said Arturo. I only used a five. Ay, that Ray, said Lilia's sister who overheard. And Tonio was being very good here at the reception, not a sound. Look how much money they have on them now, Lilia, said Arturo, what a honeymoon they will have with that. Boy what we could do with the money. Shh, said Lilia. Delia and Mario were full of other people's kisses, too. Even the air was full of the kisses that missed. Yuk, said Tonio. Yuk, said Jorge, like my grandmother. Ray was yelling for another beer. No one would give it to him.

What do you mean? *Ya cálmate* Ray, come on, said Jaime. So? Come on Ray, don't be like that, brother, said Mario. Ray winked at Delia. The mariachis were leaving and Los Lovers were setting up to take over again.

"Come on, Jorge, it's time," said Tonio. They didn't have any dollars so they had come up with something just as good. Not the present, exactly. Bullets. They each had one in their pockets. These would be their dollars, their dance.

Everyone watched them. So cute, and wasn't he the one.... It was the first time either one had gotten out of his seat tonight. And they were, after all, celebrities. Sort of. Everyone followed them, every pair of eyes. Ray saw them. He stopped shouting for beer. He put his hands on his hips. He shouted something different.

"Well, lookit, lookit who's coming." He pointed. "It's little mudder and farter!"

It was too funny, and the timing was too perfect. The room took one big breath and laughed one big laugh and didn't stop. It sounded like in the cave, but these were strangers.

Tonio ran for the presents' table, for the silver-flecked present. Jorge looked at Mario and pulled out his bullet. "It's a gun. For you. And this bullet, too. They were the only things we had to give you."

"A gun?" Mario yelled, but quietly in that way people can, "wait, Tonio!"

Ray stood there looking, nothing sinking in anymore. Laughter was enough for him.

Why me, said Delia's mother.

Tonio grabbed the packet and ripped it open. He stopped for just a second and wiped water from his eyes and noise from his ears. He loaded the bullet into the gun, like before. It had never worked. It had to work now. He didn't know if the bullet was in the right place, exactly. He ran back toward Mario and Jorge and Ray. And Ray.

"Tonio, hey, what's that, man?" said Mario, stepping in between Tonio and Ray. "Looks like a wedding present. Is it?"

"Yes," said Tonio. He stood there. Everyone stood there, every pair of eyes.

"Hey, a gun, wow!" It was big in Tonio's hands.

Tonio stood there.

"Oh, and hey, it's a blank gun, like a cap gun—why didn't you tell me? And Jorge says there are two bullets, well, I guess they're really blanks, no? Just for the noise. Thank you, guys."

Ray fell to the floor drunk.

"What did you guys do," said Mario looking at the rust on the gun—*it was not a blank gun*—"find this thing?" He went over and took it. He tousled Tonio's hair. He tousled Jorge's hair. He looked at the engaged safety. Jesus.

Tonio looked at Jorge. Who looked back at Tonio. Not even a real gun? But it looked like a gun, just like one. Didn't it Jorge? If only we had tried it. We should have tried it. So stupid not to. Jorge?

Jorge farted. The room, the world stopped. Jorge? Every couple somehow found itself, and held on. The boys went to each other, and looked up, at everyone in the room. Everyone coming toward them.

Why me, why me? said Delia's mother. Said Tonio's mother.

The Secret Lion

I was twelve and in junior high school and something happened that we didn't have a name for, but it was there nonetheless like a lion, and roaring, roaring that way the biggest things do. Everything changed. Just that. Like the rug, the one that gets pulled—or better, like the tablecloth those magicians pull where the stuff on the table stays the same but the gasp! from the audience makes the staying-the-same part not matter. Like that.

What happened was there were teachers now, not just one teacher, teach-erz, and we felt personally abandoned somehow. When a person had all these teachers now, he didn't get taken care of the same way, even though six was more than one. Arithmetic went out the door when we walked in. And we saw girls now, but they weren't the same girls we used to know because we couldn't talk to them anymore, not the same way we used to, certainly not to Sandy, even though she was my neighbor, too. Not even to her. She just played the piano all the time. And there were words, oh there were words in junior high school, and we wanted to know what they were, and how a person did them—that's what school was supposed to be for. Only, in junior high school, school wasn't school, everything was backward-like. If you went up to a teacher and said the word to try and find out what it meant you got in trouble for saying it. So we didn't. And we figured it must have been that way about other stuff, too, so we never said anything about anything—we weren't stupid.

But my friend Sergio and I, we solved junior high school. We would come home from school on the bus, put our books away, change shoes, and go across the highway to the arroyo. It was the one place we were not supposed to go. So we did. This was, after all, what junior high had at least shown us. It was our river, though, our personal Mississippi, our friend from long back, and it was full of stories and all the branch forts we had built in it when we were still the Vikings of America, with our own symbol, which we had carved everywhere, even in the sand, which let the water take it. That was good, we had decided; whoever was at the end of this river would know about us.

At the very very top of our growing lungs, what we would do down there was shout every dirty word we could think of, in every combination we could come up with, and we would yell about girls, and all the things we wanted to do with them, as loud as we could—we didn't know what we wanted to do with them, just things—and we would yell about teachers, and how we loved some of them, like Miss Crevelone, and how we wanted to dissect some of them, making signs of the cross, like priests, and we would yell this stuff over and over because it felt good, we couldn't explain why, it just felt good and for the first time in our lives there was nobody to tell us we couldn't. So we did.

One Thursday we were walking along shouting this way, and the railroad, the Southern Pacific, which ran above and along the far side of the arroyo, had dropped a grinding ball down there, which was, we found out later, a cannonball thing used in mining. A bunch of them were put in a big vat which turned around and crushed the ore. One had been dropped, or thrown—what do caboose men do when they get bored— but it got down there regardless and as we were walking along yelling about one girl or another, a particular Claudia, we found it, one of these things, looked at it, picked it up, and got very very excited, and held it and passed it back and forth, and we were saying "Guythisis, this is, geeGuythis...": we had this perception about nature then, that nature is imperfect and that round things are perfect: we said "GuyGodthis is perfect, thisisthis is perfect, it's round, round and heavy, it'sit's the best thing we'veeverseen. Whatisit?" We didn't know. We just knew it was great. We just, whatever, we played with it, held it some more.

And then we had to decide what to do with it. We knew, because of a lot of things, that if we were going to take this and show it to anybody, this discovery, this best thing, was going to be taken away from us. That's the way it works with little kids, like all the polished quartz, the tons of it we had collected piece by piece over the years. Junior high kids too. If we took it home, my mother, we knew, was going to look at it and say "throw that dirty thing in the, get rid of it." Simple like, like that. "But ma it's the best thing I" "Getridofit." Simple.

So we didn't. Take it home. Instead, we came up with the answer. We dug a hole and we buried it. And we marked it secretly. Lots of secret signs. And came back the next week to dig it up and, we didn't know, pass it around some more or something, but we didn't find it. We dug up that whole bank, and we never found it again. We tried.

99

Sergio and I talked about that ball or whatever it was when we couldn't find it. All we used were small words, neat, good. Kid words. What we were really saying, but didn't know the words, was how much that ball was like that place, that whole arroyo: couldn't tell anybody about it, didn't understand what it was, didn't have a name for it. It just felt good. It was just perfect in the way it was that place, that whole going to that place, that whole junior high school lion. It was just iron-heavy, it had no name, it felt good or not, we couldn't take it home to show our mothers, and once we buried it, it was gone forever.

The ball was gone, like the first reasons we had come to that arroyo years earlier, like the first time we had seen the arroyo, it was gone like everything else that had been taken away. This was not our first lesson. We stopped going to the arroyo after not finding the thing, the same way we had stopped going there years earlier and headed for the mountains. Nature seemed to keep pushing us around one way or another, teaching us the same thing every place we ended up. Nature's gang was tough that way, teaching us stuff.

When we were young we moved away from town, me and my family. Sergio's was already out there. Out in the wilds. Or at least the new place seemed like the wilds since everything looks bigger the smaller a man is. I was five, I guess, and we had moved three miles north of Nogales where we had lived, three miles north of the Mexican border. We looked across the highway in one direction and there was the arroyo; hills stood up in the other direction. Mountains, for a small man.

When the first summer came the very first place we went to was of course the one place we weren't supposed to go, the arroyo. We went down in there and found water running, summer rain water mostly, and we went swimming. But every third or fourth or fifth day, the sewage treatment plant that was, we found out, upstream, would release whatever it was that it released, and we would never know exactly what day that was, and a person really couldn't tell right off by looking at the water, not every time, not so a person could get out in time. So, we went swimming that summer and some days we had a lot of fun. Some days we didn't. We found a thousand ways to explain what happened on those other days, constructing elaborate stories about the neighborhood dogs, and hadn't she, my mother, miscalculated her step before, too? But she knew something was up because we'd come running into the house those days, wanting to take a shower, even—if this can be imagined—in the middle of the day.

That was the first time we stopped going to the arroyo. It taught us to look the other way. We decided, as the second side of summer came, we wanted to go into the mountains. They were still mountains then. We went running in one summer Thursday morning, my friend Sergio and I, into my mother's kitchen, and said, well, what'zin, what'zin those hills over there—we used her word so she'd understand us—and she said nothingdon'tworryaboutit. So we went out, and we weren't dumb, we thought with our eyes to each other, ohhoshe'stryingtokeepsomethingfromus. We knew adult.

We had read the books, after all; we knew about bridges and castles and wildtreacherousraging alligatormouth rivers. We wanted them. So we were going to go out and get them. We went back that morning into that kitchen and we said "We're going out there, we're going into the hills, we're going away for three days, don't worry." She said, "All right."

"You know," I said to Sergio, "if we're going to go away for three days, well, we ought to at least pack a lunch."

But we were two young boys with no patience for what we thought at the time was mom-stuff: making sa-and-wiches. My mother didn't offer. So we got our little kid knapsacks that my mother had sewn for us, and into them we put the jar of mustard. A loaf of bread. Knivesforksplates, bottles of Coke, a can opener. This was lunch for the two of us. And we were weighed down, humped over to be strong enough to carry this stuff. But we started walking, anyway, into the hills. We were going to eat berries and stuff otherwise. "Goodbye." My mom said that.

After the first hill we were dead. But we walked. My mother could still see us. And we kept walking. We walked until we got to where the sun is straight overhead, noon. That place. Where that is doesn't matter; it's time to eat. The truth is we weren't anywhere close to that place. We just agreed that the sun was overhead and that it was time to eat, and by tilting our heads a little we could make that the truth.

"We really ought to start looking for a place to eat."

"Yeah. Let's look for a good place to eat." We went back and forth saying that for fifteen minutes, making it lunchtime because that's what we always said back and forth before lunchtimes at home. "Yeah, I'm hungry all right." I nodded my head. "Yeah, I'm hungry all right too. I'm hungry." He nodded his head. I nodded my head back. After a good deal more nodding, we were ready, just as we came over a little hill. We hadn't found the mountains yet. This was a little hill.

And on the other side of this hill we found heaven.

It was just what we thought it would be.

Perfect. Heaven was green, like nothing else in Arizona. And it wasn't a cemetary or like that because we had seen cemetaries and they had gravestones and stuff and this didn't. This was perfect, had trees, lots of trees, had birds, like we had never seen before. It was like "The Wizard of Oz," like when they got to Oz and everything was so green, so emerald, they had to wear those glasses, and we ran just like them, laughing, laughing that way we did that moment, and we went running down to this clearing in it all, hitting each other that good way we did.

We got down there, we kept laughing, we kept hitting each other, we unpacked our stuff, and we started acting "rich." We knew all about how to do that, like blowing on our nails, then rubbing them on our chests for the shine. We made our sandwiches, opened our Cokes, got out the rest of the stuff, the salt and pepper shakers. I found this particular hole and I put my coke right into it, a perfect fit, and I called it my Coke-holder. I got down next to it on my back, because everyone knows that rich people eat lying down, and I got my sandwich in one hand and put my other arm around the Coke in its holder. When I wanted a drink, I lifted my neck a little, put out my lips, and tipped my Coke a little with the crook of my elbow. Ah.

We were there, lying down, eating our sandwiches, laughing, throwing bread at each other and out for the birds. This was heaven. We were laughing and we couldn't believe it. My mother *was* keeping something from us, ah ha, but we had found her out. We even found water over at the side of the clearing to wash our plates with—we had brought plates. Sergio started washing his plates when he was done, and I was being rich with my Coke, and this day in summer was right.

When suddenly these two men came, from around a corner of trees and the tallest grass we had ever seen. They had bags on their backs, leather bags, bags and sticks.

We didn't know what clubs were, but I learned later, like I learned about the grinding balls. The two men yelled at us. Most specifically, one wanted me to take my Coke out of my Coke-holder so he could sink his golf ball into it.

Something got taken away from us that moment. Heaven. We grew up a little bit, and couldn't go backward. We learned. No one had ever told us about golf. They had told us about heaven. And it went away. We got golf in exchange.

We went back to the arroyo for the rest of that summer, and tried to have fun the best we could. We learned to be ready for finding the grinding ball. We loved it, and when we buried it we knew what would happen. The truth is, we didn't look so hard for it. We were two boys and twelve summers then, and not stupid. Things get taken away.

We buried it because it was perfect. We didn't tell my mother, but together it was all we talked about, till we forgot. It was the lion.

Eyes Like They Say The Devil Has

My mother had always been too impatient. When I was still at an age when I couldn't dress myself properly, my mother was not much help. She would always forget about dressing me until the last moment, and then I would walk out of the house with socks pulled up to my tiny hips and sometimes over, compliments of that lady. She could not even wait for the next day, any next day, and since it never came I'm not sure she ever did have any life of her own to speak of when she wasn't out of breath. The signs of her inability to wait were numerous, but small and insidious, so many that after awhile none of us ever paid her any attention, not with regard to her "don't be silly, mom" problem.

But the signs were there just the same: she would, for example, become thoroughly useless, almost limp, for at least an hour before the mail would come. Nothing would get done besides her pacing, or her sitting down and getting up, even though all she ever got that was hers was miniscule and joyless, bills, you-live-here-it's-yours-lady mail, secret sales at Penney's. Forget holidays when the mail didn't come, especially those holidays that don't sound like holidays so that one might harbor a suspicion about mail delivery, all of us knowing that post office phones never get answered. And when she had her coffee in the morning she stood by the kettle until it screamed—not that first little blip-spit whoopee cushion start, but the full Alfred Hitchcock thing. We had a cuckoo clock, too, and every five minutes before it cuckooed, well. And Christmas, ah, we sang a lot in December.

All of which lends some logic to why, when I was celebrating my tenth birthday, my mother wondered out loud what I would be like when I was twenty. Let me capitalize the word wonder. And she liked even numbers—they gave her a sense of symmetry, balancing her, I guess. I never could explain it, either, but she chose my tenth birthday anyway. As I blew out the candles I could tell that the fire itself had not gone out; I had blown it into my mother's eyes, which only she could hold there in that way of hers without her eyes melting all down and dripping like the cake icing onto one of those cake plates. She told me years later that that was the moment she decided to take me to Madre Sofía. I already knew.

Grown-ups are like that, somehow. They *decide*. That's all. Kids, on the other hand, *wish*. I never did learn to become invisible at will, which is what I wanted at that moment as I blew. If I had just *decided* to become invisible, the world might have been an altogether different place, since deciding is stronger. But it's a conspiracy among grown-ups to keep that power out of tiny hands, to relegate super hero stuff to comic books. "Make a wish," they say. It would be just too scary to say "make a decision." That's why we say wishy-washy, and never decidey-washy. That is a harsh fact, deciding being stronger than wishing. But a fact is a fact, so they say, and that's what one learns at a gypsy's, contrary to popular notion.

I must tell you, then, that gypsies live in regular houses. Yes, of course, they decorate them differently, but basically they have places with four walls and all the other stuff. This gypsy, anyway. Add a thousand mirrors, paint everything in black, dead-sky blue, and maroon, and stuff up the chimney so that there's smoke everywhere and yeek, there is Madre Sofía's, the place my mother took me after she *decided*. Took me by the hand, I might add, and quickly, even with my socks up to my hips, so that we looked like an ambitious kid trying to get his clumsy box kite up into the air, the kite making only a half-hearted effort so it kind of bounces. I was not the kid.

Reasons for haste, however, are always complicated, never singular. My mother was in a hurry for other reasons besides just wanting to know what I'd be like in ten years (the answer to that question at that moment would have been easy: dead from flying too low and smashing into a wall full of Spanish graffiti, a dot over the large i of some obscenity). But let me tell you about this lady, this Madre Sofía, who was the one rumored to have been responsible for that little baby in a box all wrapped up and decorated and put into the pile of gifts at the Gonzalez wedding a couple of years back. That was a real kicker. They opened the presents that night, which was lucky or not, because the baby might have suffocated. They never did pin it on her. I'm not even sure how or why she was involved, but she was. All she ever said about it was "every baby has a family." That didn't answer the question, of course, and not a whole lot of people have wanted to be seen with her since. "Gypsies," they said, even though she'd been there as long as I knew, and went about as far as the grocery. Her answer didn't do me much good, either. All I wanted to know, since I had just found out about this word at the time, was whether or not the poor baby would be a bastard, and would he get to inherit any of those presents they got. Kings' bastards didn't, unless there was a lot of blood, and I sensed a story here, but no one would talk.

So we hurried. Not to be invisible as much as to know all about the future. Now all this commotion is not to say that we put on Groucho disguises or anything, though I think my mother was not above it with the way we were all dressed up in winter clothes even though the spring heat in Arizona that year was like plastic wrap all over our bodies. Finally, we reached a small screened porch with a hand-made "Walk in" sign on the outside, so we did. Just like that. My mother let out one of her burden-of-the-universe sighs, even though we could be seen plain as anything through the screen. Things are funny that way. This Sofía was such a horror nobody was even supposed to look at this place for fear of measles or contagious leprosy, so once we were on the porch, poof—we were invisible. If only I had known it at the time, but no. I didn't yet have the knack of the art, the proper sophistication. That wishing and deciding thing again.

As we got in, the real front door to the house was open, but the doorway was covered with some heavy maroon curtains which had a kind of grandmother lace sewn over them. A little bell sounded somewhere, like at the Chinese grocery. Actually, it sounded somewhere behind the curtains; there was a laundry-line cord attached to the door and running through the doorway at the top center, right where the curtains met. The curtains were fraying there, especially.

I expected certain things, I suppose—wishing goes hand in hand with dreaming—and some of them were there. I expected the mirrors, and of course the dark colors and all that stuff. But there wasn't a cloud of smoke on the ground. It did smell of cigarettes, but that was the closest thing. No smoke like in television dreams, the way a person passes out and starts walking anyway. And there wasn't any of that music like at the Italian pizza house. As we waited we could hear the sound of someone, or something—I wasn't ruling out surprises yet—in a back room, sometimes, but that was it. Nothing else was particularly noticeable.

Except Madre Sofía. Gypsy. *Gitana.* Again I thought I had known what to expect, more or less. I had heard talk—not the men's talk, they always made me go away. But the women's. And the school bus passed by her house, and I had seen her from a distance, emptying garbage behind the carport or getting into her old car with the blankets all over it. But *from a distance* is a long way from *from a doorway.* She walked in, and everything was hers. That's how I felt, as if my tongue wasn't mine, as if I knew I wouldn't be able to talk, as if other parts of me weren't mine, even my clothes. That feeling.

Not that I was scared, exactly; people get scared of things they don't know anything about. She was familiar in a hundred different ways—she just put those ways together funny. *That* was scary. Like the big man, the prisoner with the black beard who got away from the county jail that day, or my cousin the UnIted STAtes MaRINE who made the pieces of a jigsaw puzzle fit, and nobody said anything. From behind the maroon curtain, in a very high, but not squeaky, voice, she said come in, I think. I didn't hear.

I saw. As we walked into the room through the curtains, which turned out to be awful heavy, she was sitting at a dining room table and cocked her head up, a head that looked like a loose jar top on plum jam, half turned and not caught properly in the threads the way my mother always yelled at me for. It was like a fake head, no joke, like a jar top too big or too small for the jar. Or even more I've got it, she was like my friend's brother smiling, as he hit himself. He got his smiles and his crying all mixed up. But they said *he* was retarded.

And in that head, maybe because of makeup—sometimes my mother used too much in a hurry, and she messed up, too—she was growing flowers. Poppies. Dull, yellowish poppies on her mahogany face, right around her eyes. And when I looked, because I couldn't help it, at her eyes, they were half yellow and half gray at the same time, maybe from the light, but yellow eyes like they say the devil has, like a goat. But gray, too. A fancy goat, a dressed-up goat. Devil in a tweed suit. And giant red lips (I wasn't too surprised—I'd seen those on my mother, too). And the smell of smoke that the house had was coming from her, I guess she had been smoking, but it was diamond smoke, somehow. It was as if mineral water turned into smoke and I inhaled the sparkles, but dry, and I could feel them in my throat, and then I really had to breathe, and I could feel sparkles in my stomach. And she was fat, but the fat was almost invisible. I knew right away she was fat because of the way she moved her lips—almost as if she were making fun, they moved in and out over and over as if she were always kissing. Real fat people do that, even if they have all their teeth.

She didn't speak, and as a child I could only answer, because that's all a kid can do when being polite, and my mother surely told me about being polite today. So, together, we were silent, cold and wet, dry and hard—everything all at once. Or at least I felt that way. As if I had gotten caught, but I didn't do anything even if no one would believe me. I was going to cross myself, this felt more and more like church, if only to have something for my hands to do—and when is crossing yourself ever impolite, I thought. But at that moment, from behind, my mother pushed me forward, and she was bigger than I was then, so my body moved. I felt like a sacrifice. Mom was aces some days.

And then. This lady put her hand on the poked-out face of a thin animal wrap, tossing that head behind her, pressuring it incredibly as she sat back in the huge chair and leaned. Just leaned. At that moment the face might have been mine. But I knew it wasn't; I was still looking at her, while that other face, that animal other face, ex-face, was somewhere in the folds of her back. She had probably first worn it alive, around her neck like skinny old ladies sometimes let cats lie, only she never heard it scream when.... I couldn't think about it. I decided to say something about having such a nice chair at a dining room table.

Of course somewhere in my head it made sense, she must have spent a lot of time there, mostly with a fork, but at that razor-point moment I saw her chest—chests, each as large as her head. Folded together, coming out of her dress as if it didn't fit, not like my mother's anyway. I could see them, how she kept them penned up, leisurely, loosely, in maroon feed bags, horse nuzzles of her wide body. Horse nuzzles. Horses always came over to me, kind of nuzzling me, sticking their long snout-nose-mouths into my chest so I'd hand over the sugar cube. Maybe this happened to her, only two horses did it, and she gave them karate chops just below the eyes and walked off with the two nuzzles. Or maybe she got them like she got that fur, somehow. It didn't matter. There they were, penned up, now, fancy, circled by pearl reins and red scarves. Hiding teeth, maybe. I didn't want to hear about it.

But aside from all that, as I finally took my first breath—which must have sounded like Jack LaLanne deep-breathing—there wasn't much else. Or I couldn't take my eyes off her to look, I don't know exactly which. And she didn't take her eyes off me. She lifted her arm, which was obvious work—and showed me she meant business, I could tell, God, she had seen me looking at her chests—but only with the tips of her fingers motioned me to sit opposite. She couldn't have yelled louder and I couldn't have said "Yes ma'am" faster than I sat. When she opened her mouth (or really, one of the continuous times she opened her mouth), the voice was not the one that had told us to come in. Hoarsely, she spoke obviously to my mother—where was she all this time, old pal—but looked directly at me. Little, thin, holy at this moment as never before, attentive me, who heard the words come dark, smoky like the small room smelled, dark smoke, words coming like red ants stepping occasionally from a hole on a summer day in the valley. The words whatever they were seemed to dribble from those kissing lips, as if she hated to give them up but had too many, so quiet it was hard to tell where they came from, red ants from her mouth, her nose, her ears, then tears from the corners of her cinched eyes. It was the tears, I think. I was certainly convinced. She could have been reciting my own mother's recipe for enchiladas. I hadn't heard even one word, or I didn't understand, but I had seen ants. That much was absolute. Hoarse, dark-red ants.

When suddenly she put her hand full on my head, my tiny head, pinching tight with those same fingertips like a television healer, like Oral Roberts young on that Sunday show. My cataracts would disappear. But actually, that's all I really could do at that moment was see. She would have to heal me of my hearing loss, then, and feeling and speaking and breathing. I hadn't yet taken a second breath. This was the most exciting thing that had ever been in my life. Read "scared to death" for the word "exciting." I was a sinner getting to walk in an Oral Roberts line, finally reaching Him. Only it was Her.

I remember how Oral Roberts would then suddenly get those inspired bursts of rocket energy, and he'd push those people's heads down like a vigilante jailer, making them kneel, chins almost to the floor, and he'd say a thousand words like a holy machine gun. Well jeez I don't know how she made it across that dining room table, what with her tonnage—maybe it was a reaching-for-a-second-helping motion, or maybe the animal wrap had been waiting for this moment to bite back—but half standing, quickly, buzz saw quick, half leaning the distance, swinging those nuzzles toward me, she *got* that hand on my head, and I reached down with both my hands even faster to my lap, protecting instinctively whatever it is that needs protection when a baseball is thrown and you're not looking but someone yells.

That hand, then that chest coming toward me like the quarterarms of the amputee Joaquín who came back from the war to sit in the park. He'd reach out at all the kids when none of the grown-ups was watching, and we all knew about it, and dreamed about it, and one day he was caught, and he had to be held back and we never saw him again. I sat there, no breath, and could see, my head held down and me trying hard to lift it, what? Hair around, you should excuse me, her left chest, like a man. Like my father's, I thought. That's all I could see, that's all there was to see, straight down into the feed bags. Except too that her clothes were old, like the curtains on the doorway.

I sat forced back in my chair. I closed my eyes and felt a particular pain different from her fingertips which, don't make any mistake, were hurting, too. I was slouched—not on purpose, thank you mother and thank you for being in a fireman's rush to rescue me wherever you were—and was sitting right on that stupid knot that jeans have in back, low in back which anyone knows who's done sit-ups or anything like

108

that. Everything was blurring. This was all I could feel. She—I don't mean my mother—spoke to me now.

All accented, in a language whose spine had been snapped, she whispered the singularly recognizable words of a city witch, and made me happy, finally, if one can understand it, alive like a man. "The future will make you tall." That was it. Or that was the only thing I heard. The whole time. That and the laugh as we were on the way out, a small laugh but one that couldn't wait. My mother paid her, thanked her, attempted to shake her hand, and we left. Running, almost. My mother had gotten what she came for. Or I hoped she had—I sure wasn't ever coming back.

Of course, the future didn't. I wonder about my birthday wish that year, the one about wanting to be invisible. If only it had been a *decision*. I think going to see this Sofía was maybe that wish coming true as well as it possibly could—we had, after all, been invisible for the moment. And now I had *I was going to be tall* to take home with me. All from a lady in a dining room, a dining room of all things, who made us happy, somehow. Scared us into happiness, happy even to be leaving, But happy. And that was the trick.

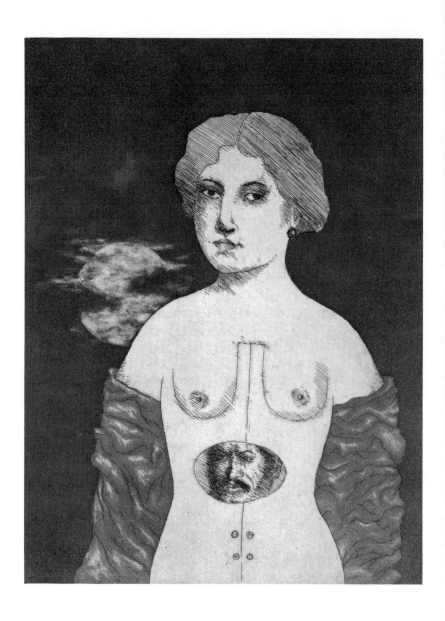

The Birthday
of Mrs. Pineda

Café Combate, ¡la gente toma!
Café Combate, ¡de rica aroma!

—a famous, and old, commercial jingle run on the radio in
Mexico for many years, advertising a particular brand of coffee.
It ran repeatedly, obsessively, and no one who heard it has been
able to forget.

Café Combate, the people drink it!
Café Combate, such rich aroma!

The noise came through the mouth of his nose: "hummph."

Adolfo Pineda had read the books on El Salvador, but they didn't
matter. He understood them, all right—which is to say, he understood
that he did not understand them. So he kept reading them, buying them,
rereading them, shrugging his shoulders. He read them everywhere, all
the time; the names were so familiar, so like his. He read them at dinner:
a page turned, a mouthful of *chilaquiles;* a page, a napkin to his lips in a
wipe of the sauce. At the part about the genitals in men's mouths, he
thought twice before chewing, but only twice. Truly believing such a
story would mean no dinner. Conscience is like that.

"Fito," his wife called at him. She was always young when she called
him like this, like the wind, which goes away but comes back again and is
recognized easily. They had met at thirteen, when he was still Adolfito,
and she was then his Mariquita.

111

"Fito!"

"*Sí sí sí sí*, what."

"Stop reading." She looked at the newest magazine. Dead children again on the cover. Dead and flat, the way magazine covers make them, so they cannot be touched, so that a hand cannot go under the head. "You said you would. So much blood and screaming, I can hear it all the way over in the kitchen. Close that story. You said you would, you promised. Read me about the Prince and *ésa, la Diana,* read me about that baby. You said you would." She cleared his dishes away.

"Mari..."

"No, no coffee. Or Sanka. You want that, Sanka?"

"Ay, Mari. Give me coffee."

"Give me give me give me. If I had known..."

"What? If you had known what?"

"Give me give me. Thirty years ago, if I had known what would happen, what you...."

Adolfo Pineda clicked his teeth to break her sentence in half. "Oh stop it. Come on, *m'ija,* it's just coffee, that's all I want. Chh. It's not going to keep me awake." María Pineda looked at him. Inside, behind her eyes, she saw the old radio and hummed the jingle that took her back to all the lunch times of her growing up, to all the rice and ground beef meals she ate hearing it. She ate the music of the old coffee jingle with her ears, chewed it over and over

Café Combate, ¡la gente toma!
Café Combate, ¡de rica aroma!

all of it came back for the five seconds of humming that she took, then went back inside her. She wanted to give him coffee. Very strong, very black, *cariculillo, Tapachula,* or even the *Café Combate* of the song; for so many years they had kept it in their cups. They had taken it out of the thin, brown paper bags. He loved it, and she loved him to love it. Something for her about a man liking something passionately, anything, boxing even, something about it made her give in to anything.

"But the doctor, you know..."

"It won't hurt, and I'm not going to tell him."

María Pineda clicked her teeth at him and went to get the coffee. Humming. He got it three nights out of seven and sometimes twice in a night if he read to her about good things. He was a lion when he read. His roaring came from so many years of the politics and smoke, of reading the smudged and crowded newsprints of all the smallest newspapers from all the smallest countries *de abajo,* all the smallest countries down there with all the biggest names, the fat Indian names, and the names of saints.

112

But when he read to her about the good things, about Charles or about what her *tía* in San Luis Potosí wrote, he had to use his loud moments up on words like *kiss*, "...and he KISSED his wife," or bananas, so that the news was that her *tía* had gone to the market and bought BANANAS. He made it all sound so important, and María Pineda would laugh at him invariably at some juncture in the night, and he would not understand. He would wrinkle his face up like paper and throw his fine mood into the waste basket. He would stop reading to her then and go back to his books, or his magazines, El Salvador, El Salvador, or his tiny and smudged letters in newsprint for which he would need the magnifying glass. And coffee. Slyly, he would add this. "And coffee," he would say, "and leave me alone."

"Here, *m'ijo*." She set down some new coffee next to him. Its steam hands made him pay attention, pulling his head almost to its face.

"But this is only half, you didn't fill the cup...." He frowned, till there was no room left on his face for more frowning. But he managed. It was a little something extra with the left half of the left eyebrow, perhaps an added twitch of the eyelid underneath.

"It was full when I started from the kitchen. *Ni modo.*"

Hummph. He said this more with his chest than with any sounds. He let his face relax a little as he took the flirting sip. Two and a half cups in one night was the best he had done this year. And anyway, he had seen half a cup disappear before, so he was not truly angry. Coffee disappearing was nothing new, he had seen it often, even before María. It was the uncles. His mother had told him, and it was true. Even dead uncles want coffee. Coffee is not a thing a man stops wanting. Somewhere with his own hands Adolfo Pineda could even remember picking coffee beans, could remember the smell even then, the wanting. Or it was a story somebody told him about his grandfather. The feeling went too far back to be clear, so he frowned again and tried to remember for a fact what had happened, what the story was...

"Anna came over today."

"Anna?" Adolfo Pineda looked up from his reading, which was really thinking.

María Pineda looked at him looking up from his reading and felt good. But now, because he looked up, this story of Anna was going to have to be a little better than what really happened. She had him, and had to take care.

He knew that, of course. He knew it the moment he lifted his head and was sorry for the little lie he was going to make her tell him. He should have remembered to look up earlier and say something casual, anything just so that his looking up now would seem less like a lion's or a bear's. But he could feel that she had him now like a tender fish. And she had better be careful or the fish would balloon-pop! into the lion they both thought of him as, into the bear he knew he sometimes was. The thing wasn't true, but he could tell it was there between them. After thirty years a feeling like that... well, never mind, he told himself. He stopped thinking the thought. He knew it would get no clearer than the coffee beans.

Not in words, anyway. But a kind of heart that the mind has pulsed the thought through for him regardless of his trying to stop it. This second heart always troubled him like that. It didn't pay attention. No attention to decorum—that was a word from the army, or from his grandfather—the decorum with which he now tried to live his life. It leaped so very quickly back and forth between times and events, this heart, that he didn't understand. And it scared him. Thirty years were nothing, and a minute sometimes was the entire lifetime of several men back to back.

Todasbodas. That's what it was saying to him now, in that language that was not words, and not the hummph intended for María. *Todasbodas.* It was reminding him of how he used to be an *all-weddings.* It skipped through the thirty years he was sitting down with now, back to the younger bones he used to have and the different shirts and the thin black moustaches of which he took such care in every mirror that he passed.

Adolfo Pineda looked at his wife about to tell him the story of Anna's visit today, and his second heart remembered for him the time when his ambition was to swing from crystal chandeliers, to be expert in this, and to take his talent through the fanciest houses of the jungle countries, and then to Europe, to the continent, with final recognition and general applause in Paris, where they would—in his old age—offer him a pension in honor of his selfless and fine work in redefining wildness.

He looked at his wife and he smiled.

Today was her birthday. She was some age or other. She was nineteen when they married, and that was the only birthday that ever mattered to his second heart, and it only mattered because it was the first measure of her that he had. They had lived in Guaymas, the both of them then. He could remember that she was nineteen, but he could not remember the first time he had made love to her. That he could not remember is what he remembered now. Something was always indistinct to him there, about that. Like the coffee beans. What he knew now, what he remembered, was that he had known a number of girls and had told each one his story.

The story concerned a particular history of Guaymas, the *true history of Guaymas,* as he would say. It was a sham, but no more so than any other history—of Guaymas or of any other place. It was as true and as false as the things any people say to get each other's clothes off now and fast. The true history of Guaymas is told in eight separate volumes in the mayor's office, the back office, and he had read them by special permission before the fire. An intricate weave, he would say, and he hummed it like a song back to himself now, an intricate weave, the words were so familiar suddenly, not so far back, so ingrained, so like the lines on a wooden post; an intricate weave, he would say, about this traitor and that shopkeeper, some lover of stray cats and three toothless women; but in truth there was no general who did *that,* not ever, not anywhere. Only in his words. Adolfo Pineda told the story to impress some Mariquita, this Mariquita this time, and it worked, God, it worked, so it had to be real, this story, because it was the thing that got her print dress and thin shoes to come off, this story of himself as the youngest general with thin moustaches and a cape who, with his singleness of arm strength, pushed the difficult song of violence farther than the rest, but on the right side of things. At this the girls sighed with relief, sure that a man on the right side of things could not be wrong.

But it must have been the business of saving the six Sisters of Mercy against which this Catholic Mariquita could not win—none of them could win here; she could only melt like sugars into the arm of this particular history, the one that must be true even for hard Catholic girls from the desert north, melt like sugars into the arm, into the face of a man who talked through the seasons and the seasons of the night.

María Pineda, about to tell the story of Anna's visit and wrestling around very quickly in her head for extra words to make the story better and so to keep his tender and old attention longer, saw Adolfo Pineda smile at her.

Just smile at her.

He had not done that, not like that, since before, since the far before. He still smiled at her, but his smiles were embers, now, not strong quick wood fires. They were warmer now, and more lasting, but his smiles no longer held a sense of danger, that they might burn, that they might reach off his face and stretch in some lightning bolt fist straight at her, down and through the electricity in the cells at the core of her inside self.

She had been María Elena then, daughter of the vendor of strings, strings for all occasions, and rough cotton threads, Don Miguel, and his wife, la señora Beltran, who never smiled and so was never addressed by her first name.

But her Fito was smiling at her now, and she was standing in the time when he had called her by the names of various imported perfumes taken, he would say, from the wildest flowers of the wilted and perfect bouquets found in subtle crystal vases set on absurd tables in one particular back street bistro in springtime Paris just the year before.

He said this, but it said nothing about what he would do. From that moment she could never disentwine her other memory of the time of perfumes, that time just after they had married when she had to go looking for him, had to step over a dried phlegm and dirt floor in a dark cock-fighting barn, had to step over this floor made of sputum from half-shaved, thick men and dying cocks, a floor bloodstained and scuffed into a kind of inexpert, misshapen setting of scab tiles. The sounds of the fight would not go away, the sounds of all those men huddled, nor the odor of that perfume, and she remembered how she had seen as she ran by the one soul-white cock splattered with blood like grease, hot, how it had an eye pulled clean out but continued to fight, and then lost the other eye, but continued to fight, stretching its head and neck up higher and higher, imagining that something must be blocking its view, trying to see, and trying higher to see, but never for a moment thinking that it was blind. The owners kept spraying the fighter birds with water from their mouths, spitting a mist, cooling and cooling, fooling them, until the winner, the not-white one, allowed itself to be cooled and soothed and rewarded, and the owner, who was laughing, took its head into his mouth, cooling him.

María Pineda ran by them all, that perfume, into the rooms behind the barn, into one room of particular use, and she pulled Adolfo Pineda physically out of another woman and dragged him drunk home.

"Why are you smiling at me?"

"It's your birthday. Did you think I had forgotten?"

María Pineda clicked her teeth at him. "Don't you want to hear about Anna?"

"What about Anna, well. Tell me."

"She came over today."

"I know that."

"Fito! Stop it and let me tell you."

116

Again she called him by that name, and again she was young for him because of it. He liked the sound of the name as it came from her, even when she was angry. This was the second time at least tonight that she had called him that. Adolfo Pineda knew that his wife was thinking about her birthday then. She felt young, too, he could tell. He smiled even more, and she turned around and said she wasn't going to tell him the story because he wasn't paying any attention to her, not the right kind, that he was being silly. *Yes,* he thought, she was being young and he liked it. He could be young, too, for her birthday: he ignored her.

He went back to his coffee and this newest article on El Salvador. This is crazy, he thought, and this thought about the bodies with names like his took him away from his wife again. María Pineda went to the kitchen to cry. This is crazy, he thought.

"This is crazy," he said to the kitchen. Adolfo Pineda did not mean the killing and suffering, but that people would go there to see it and talk about it. Words. In a flat paper magazine. He put his hand over the picture of a line of shoeless bodies, piled in a half-hearted way. Nothing. He could feel nothing. Slick on his fingers.

He took a drink of coffee, long like a breath in the mountains. This, he thought, *this*. Coffee, from Colombia and Paraguay and there and there and there, from all the small places *de abajo*. It comes from the dirt, straight up, from hell to heaven. I drink it, he thought, and it's a way of remembering something, it reminds me to remember. Black like the earth and all its shades. It is knowing what it is to be dead, to have disappeared, to have gone. Just gone. Knowing what being dead is—this keeps us alive. Coffee makes me jump, thought Adolfo Pineda, makes me full with the spirit of wanting to do things, full with energy, with being young, full with the fear of being dead, of just lying there. Caffeine...

Hummpjh. He said this with his chest, again, bigger than with words, and rounder. No such thing exists, *caffeine*. The word is a failure, or its definition not yet finished. He could not find in any dictionary— after the doctor had told him about the word—anything about its being what it was: a power from the muscles of the dead, their backs and forearms, their dreams, and how they still want to do things, a kind of leftover need, yes, *seguro que sí*, the power of intentions never met, such strong intentions, and so many, that they could not go away. Coffee reminded him that he was alive, and would keep him alive, too, not make him one of those bodies, not like the doctor had said. These dead, they never speak in words, he thought, only whimpered, but the dead were out there. One could hear them in the wind, usually very quiet, a little irritating, but quiet, no real words. The dead have a humble streak a mile long, but not him, not Adolfo Pineda. And not his wife, either—he would not let her.

"What are you doing in there, *m'ija?*" He called to her. This being young, this way, this way of ignoring her, but paying attention that she knew he was ignoring her, was maybe no good, but what could he do. This was the only way he knew. The dead, the energy, the slow electricity of caffeine, they gave him force, but no answers. She would stop crying.

He looked at the pictures again. This was his dessert, he guessed; he hadn't asked if she had made a cake. In a minute I'll ask her, he thought. When she stops crying.

The pictures. The whole thing of them, the way they were, so flat, so dimensionless, the way they were not really the dead people at all—was like doctors. If a person goes in bleeding, the doctors fix the cut but never ask the attacker what made him stab a man, never get the *vato* in, get him in with his knife and ask how his father could let him do such a thing to someone else. Then they should rough up that knifer a little. That's what's wrong with them: these new doctors see only blood. Even *ese* doctor, *¿cómo se llama? el doctor* Martinez. He at least should know better. At least him. He came from Guaymas, too, but maybe he's too young to know the world. At least he asks a question now and then about what the kitchen knife felt like, asks that of a husband, or about how many links and how heavy they were in the hoodlum's chain that did this or that to a face.

"Did you see these pictures, *m'ija?* Did you see them? El Salvador, *otra vez.* They can't get enough. What ever happened, what about this boy that was shot, *¿cómo se llamaba*—Casillas? Remember his face? Who ever talked about him, right here in Phoenix?

"Are you all right, *m'ija?*

"A gun and blood and by strangers and everything. Everything all wrapped up in one boy's body. A man. Remember him? But it doesn't count. Maybe with presidents it counts."

Adolfo Pineda could still hear his wife, but a little less now, in the kitchen. She was feeling better. He knew she would.

Hummamph. "Let the Anglos go there. We've already been there, huh? Let the Anglos go there—they go like flies anyway, like flies on the blood of cows. They're crazy. One stays away from a place like that. It only makes sense. But it's like dinner or something to them. They must feel good or something. I don't get it, *m'ija.*

"Are you coming out? *Mira,* look here at this ad: we can go to Baskin Robbins. I haven't forgotten. Come on?" At least he couldn't hear her crying anymore.

"So they're crazy I think. That's not where the answers are. Everybody knows that. What jokes, JOKES. Look at these PICTURES. Like a MAGNET was pulling them. It STINKS. Like when the president was

118

shot, or the POPE, or some other big guy. I don't know what will happen next."

María Pineda came out of the kitchen and sat to listen—because she liked to, like always. When he was a lion like this, everything fell away. A lion.

Hummphh. "Look at them. A president gets shot and they spend three days on television trying to explain it. Of COURSE it takes three days. There's nothing to explain. And they couldn't DO it, the *pendejos*. They CAN'T explain what has no explanation." Humnnphj. "Next time somebody's SHOT they'll take two weeks and so WHAT. They STILL won't have an answer. So what."

"It's my birthday." María Pineda looked at him. She was Mariquita, and he didn't know what to say.

"Well, tell the story then."

"What story?"

"*M'ija,* don't be *tan simple.* You know. About Anna."

"Anna?"

"*Sí-sí-sí-sí.* Come on, come on. Anna, you know, Anna?"

María Pineda began her story then, about this Anna whoever she was, and it went on in its particulars, one thing bringing up another more important than the last, some things making her cry large, toad-size tears, some things not.

Mariquita Pineda began her story on her birthday, and it went on, and on further, through the night and pushed a shoulder against lunch time of the next day.

DESIGNED BY NANCY SOLOMON
SABON TYPOGRAPHY BY TUCSON TYPOGRAPHIC SERVICES
PRINTING BY ARIZONA LITHOGRAPHERS
BINDING BY ROSWELL BOOKBINDING

About the Author... Alberto Ríos is an Assistant Professor of English at Arizona State University in Tempe. He was born in Nogales, Arizona, where he attended public schools before earning his M.F.A. in creative writing at the University of Arizona. His first book of poems, *Whispering to Fool the Wind,* won the Academy of American Poets Walt Whitman Award in 1981. *The Iguana Killer* is his first collection of short fiction. Ríos lives in Chandler, Arizona, with his wife, Maria Guadalupe, who heads one branch of the Phoenix Public Library System.